COME HOME TO CRIME

✻

John Creasey: a literary phenomenon. Author of more than five hundred books—more than anyone else alive or dead as far as the records show—he has written under ten different names. Nearly one hundred million copies of his books have been sold. They have been translated into twenty-eight languages.

Born in 1908, John Creasey has a home in Arizona, U.S.A., and a home in Wiltshire and he virtually commutes between the two. Married three times, he has three sons.

Apart from his home-to-home commuting, he has travelled extensively. Aside from writing, his great interest is politics. Founder of the *All Party Alliance*, a movement advocating government by the best men (and women) from all parties together with independents, he has fought four elections for his party.

Also in Arrow Books by John Creasey

The Black Spiders
Carriers of Death
The Children of Despair
Dangerous Journey
The Day of Disaster
Days of Danger
Dark Peril
Dead or Alive
Death by Night
Death in the Rising Sun
Death round the Corner
Double for Murder
Gateway to Escape
I Am the Withered Man
Island of Peril
A Kind of Prisoner
The League of Dark Men
The Man I Didn't Kill
Men, Maids and Murde
No Darker Crime
Panic
Redhead
Return to Adventure
Sabotage
Seven Times Seven
Shadow of Doom
The Terror Trap
Unknown Mission
Where is the Withered Man?
The Withered Man

John Creasey

Come Home to Crime

ARROW BOOKS

ARROW BOOKS LTD
3 Fitzroy Square, London W1

AN IMPRINT OF THE 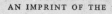 HUTCHINSON GROUP

London Melbourne Sydney Auckland
Wellington Johannesburg Cape Town
and agencies throughout the world

First published by Hurst & Blackett Ltd 1944
under John Creasey's pen-name of Norman Deane
This first, revised paperback edition
Arrow Books 1973

*Made and printed in Great Britain
by The Anchor Press Ltd,
Tiptree, Essex*
ISBN 0 09 906940 7

Contents

1

Old Enemy, New Friend?

I had a shock when I saw him standing there, sleek and well-dressed, watching the people who streamed past him through the foyer of the hotel.

I had never disliked Count Reccivi. Once I came within an ace of blowing his head off, and once he signed the order which condemned me to death. The second incident was in Rome, just before the invasion of Italy, and his German masters countermanded the order, believing that I might be a valuable source of information. The Germans, harassed and working at great pressure, were unwise enough to trust me to Italian guards, who then offered to conduct me to Allied lines if I would ensure good treatment for them as prisoners. Fantastic? Nothing like so fantastic as many of the things which have happened in Europe. If you believe that Italy swung round and joined the Allies in 1943, and you must because it is true, surely you will not question trifling incidents which seem incredible?

Reccivi was looking well, his complexion smooth and olive-skinned, his hair black and strongly—quite naturally, I think—waved. His height, five foot ten or thereabouts, was much the same as my own.

I wondered what he was doing in London. I had not grown accustomed to the fact that the Italians were 'co-belligerents', and it did not seem right to see one standing in the foyer of an English hotel.

I was waiting for Sheila, my fiancée.

I had arrived half an hour early, having finished some work with Sir Alan Clyde at the Foreign Office sooner than I expected. Outside it was cold with the crisp brightness of a late October day, but the lounge of the Chameleon was warm and comfortable enough. I lingered over my glass of beer, watching Reccivi. It was easy enough to deduce that he was expecting to see someone, even anxious that his quarry might slip through unobserved.

After ten minutes he became impatient. His gaze wandered. It rested on me for only a moment, but I saw recognition in the flick of his eyelids, before he walked out.

I stood up.

If he had acknowledged me, however distantly, I would not have worried, but it looked to me as if he was alarmed at being seen. Why should he be, unless he had some guilty reason for being in England? I did not forget that Reccivi was no longer an enemy subject, but I could not be sure that he had put all the Fascist ideas behind him. He knew me to be a British agent often assigned to special work and I knew that for some time he had directed military intelligence in Italy.

I hesitated near the door, and someone banged into me. By the time apologies had been exchanged, Reccivi had disappeared.

I strolled outside.

I need not have troubled, for it was impossible to pick an individual out of the crowds. It was midday, and every West End worker seemed to be sunning himself, and, of course, there were still hordes of servicemen in London, wearing every imaginable kind of uniform. The war was not over, although it was going well, and there was an unmistakable air of confidence and expectancy that any day would bring the news of an armistice.

I gave it up and returned to the hotel. As I did so a clock struck one, and Sheila appeared.

She brought with her, as always, the ability to make me forget about everything and everyone else. She is nearly as tall as I am, graceful, and in my eyes really lovely; it had always rather surprised me that we *are* engaged. When I discovered that she looked on me as more than the rather stolid but loyal friend of her brother, it astonished me. We had put off our marriage chiefly in deference to her mother's wishes. Perhaps I was wrong to counsel patience, but I knew that for the time being her mother would only regard me as an interloper, and I thought it better to wait until conditions were normal and I had a better chance of breaking down her family's opposition.

There were other reasons why we were not married. I was rarely in England for more than a week or two at a time. Every time I left for an assignment I went through a period of acute depression, doubting whether I would ever return. In such moments I had a horror of leaving Sheila a widow, and although the fears receded, some trace of them lingered and became the ally of Sheila's mother.

After our usual gay and light-hearted greeting Sheila turned serious and asked what had been worrying me.

Back in my mind came the encounter with Reccivi. I pushed my chair back hastily.

'I won't be five minutes,' I promised, and hurried to the telephone cubicles.

I was lucky in getting through to the Foreign Office quickly. Clyde was still there.

I told him briefly whom I had seen and what impression I had got, and rang off before he could make any comment or suggest that I should start immediately to try to find Reccivi. When I got back to the lounge Sheila was conferring with the waiter over the menu. That done, she turned to me.

'It looks as if I really made you forget something. What was it?'

I launched into the story of Reccivi. She had never met him, but his name was familiar enough. For some time she had worked in Clyde's office, leaving only because of her mother's illness. I sometimes suspected Lady St. Clare of malingering, so as to prevent Sheila from going back to London.

'So you think Reccivi thought you were watching him, and that his business here isn't straightforward.'

'I only suggest it as a possibility,' I said, cautiously. 'I'm sure of one thing: that he recognised me.'

'Every time you see a dark-haired man who might be an Italian, you get broody,' said Sheila. 'What did Clyde say?'

'I didn't give him a chance to say anything. If he wants someone to look for Reccivi, he can find a man who hasn't just come back to England and who isn't planning a fortnight with . . .'

'The loveliest girl in the world!' declared Sheila.

'Right in one!' said I. 'Darling, can you get away from Dorset for a week or so? I thought we might be able to find a quiet spot on the Devon coast.'

'It sounds heavenly.'

'Bless you!' I said, fervently.

We did not talk much over luncheon, but I think Sheila day-dreamed about a fortnight in Devon as eagerly as I did, for now and again I caught her out in a smile, and she told me that I kept grinning like a Cheshire cat. We planned to leave Waterloo by an early train next morning, and to travel light, and we decided to see a matinée that afternoon. It wasn't until we went to the lounge for coffee that she asked about Cris.

He and I, together with Anton Duval, had been on a mission which had not been without its dangers. I had come to London to make a full report while he and Anton cleared up the business.

'Do they still call him *le Liberateur*?' asked Sheila.

'Yes,' I said, 'he's very nearly a national hero. He sent his love, of course. So did Anton.'

Between Sheila and her brother there was a deep devotion. They had grown up together and saw most things the same way. Their mother, as you will have gathered, was a possessive and dominant woman, and their father in self-defence had acquired a certain vague elusiveness which did not include companionship with his children.

It would not have surprised me had Sheila hero-worshipped Cris, but in fact it was I and Anton who came nearer to doing just that. We had all three been on many desperate ventures together.

At the moment we were particularly anxious for him, for a few months before, the woman whom he had been deeply in love with had been killed, in her native France, at the hands of the retreating Germans. He had not yet recovered from the blow, but I was able to tell Sheila that he had regained the passionate interest and concentration that his work had held for him. This report cheered her up, and I had completely fogotten Reccivi when we left for the theatre.

We had tea and then parted, Sheila to the St. Clares' London house and I to my flat in Clarges Street, where I had to put the finishing touches to my reports. Before I had finished, the bell rang. Impatiently I went to the door.

The blackout restrictions were still in force and the

landing was only dimly lit; I could see only that a man was standing there. He spoke.

'I hope this is not an inconvenient time, Mr. Deane.'
The voice was that of Count Leonardo Reccivi.

2

The Apologetic Italian

'No,' I said at last, 'not at all. Come in.'

When the door was closed I saw him better. He was smiling, but there was a hint of anxiety in his expression.

'I doubt whether you expected me.'

'I didn't,' I replied. I took his hat, raincoat and gloves, put them on a chair, and led the way into the sitting-room. I left him there while I locked my papers in the desk in my study, and locked the door. When I returned he was standing in front of the electric fire.

'Will you have a drink?'

'Thank you.'

I poured him out a stiff whisky and soda, and we sat, watching each other, sipping our drinks.

'I have come to apologise for several things, Mr. Deane,' he said at last. A smile played about his expressive lips, but the hint of anxiety remained. I was puzzled. I remembered when he had sat in the tent behind the Italian lines and, after summary trial, sentenced me to death. He must have known what I was thinking, for he said quickly: 'When I learned that you had escaped,

I was genuinely pleased, but . . .' He shrugged. 'I had no alternative.'

'I know you hadn't.'

'And you harbour no feelings of hostility?'

'Not for that,' I said, brusquely.

His smile grew more strained, as he went on: 'I have to apologise for my behaviour at the Chameleon. I will not pretend that I did not recognise you. At the time you rather unnerved me.'

'So you have an uneasy conscience,' I said.

'To tell you the truth, Deane,' said Reccivi, in a more natural voice, 'I have not yet got accustomed to the fact that we are no longer enemies. We should never have been on opposite sides. I owed allegiance to my country and had no choice, but it was distasteful.'

I said stiffly: 'Well, that was the position and there was nothing we could do about it.'

'I'm glad you agree,' said Reccivi. 'I assure you I am legally entitled to be here, and my official business has the approval of your government.'

'Why *are* you here?' I demanded, bluntly.

'To supervise the repatriation of our prisoners,' said Reccivi. He gave a deprecatory smile and waved his hands. 'I like to think that my dislike of the old regime in Italy was known in London and so I was trusted with this commission.'

'You only need to recant to be forgiven,' I said, with some bitterness. There were some Italians with whom we dealt whom I thought should have stood trial for war crimes. Reccivi was not among them, and I wished I had not said it when I saw his expression. So I went on hastily: 'I once nearly killed you, so shall we take the apologies as read, and get on to whatever you've come to talk about?'

13

'What makes you think there is anything more than that?'

'For a mere exchange of civilities surely ten o'clock at night is a little late?'

Reccivi smiled. 'You may have little *finesse*, Deane, but you are difficult to deceive. I often thought that in some ways you were more dangerous than St. Clare and Duval.'

I bridled a little at the first part of the statement but in spite of myself the second part mollified me.

'Why have you come?' I demanded, brusquely. 'You stressed the fact that your official business here has been approved. Did you infer that you have private business which would not be permitted?'

'I am concerned with private business of which your government would not approve,' he said, 'or, at least, which it would not allow me to work on. I have not dared to spend time on it.'

'The last part is hard to believe,' I said.

'It is nevertheless true,' said Reccivi. 'I have freedom of movement, naturally, but I know that anything I try to do beyond the scope of my official work would be discovered and frowned upon. You see, I am suspect!'

I thought that the truth hurt him.

'All right, you're suspect,' I said, 'but why have you taken the trouble to come and tell me?'

He drew in his breath, and regarded me with narrowed eyes. I thought that he was preparing to say something that would surprise me, but I did not expect to be so flabbergasted as I was when he said:

'I think you might be able to do what I can't do.'

I stared at him, open-mouthed.

'Are you serious?'

'Of course I am serious—very much so.' He leaned

forward. 'You are just the man, Deane, and it is something that would appeal to you and to St. Clare. True, I did not think of that until I saw you at lunch-time. Since then I have given it a great deal of thought. Please! Don't refuse until you have heard more about it.'

I pulled myself together.

'Look here, Reccivi, I am answerable for everything I do to my department. You know that as well as I do. Even if I were free to act as I liked, I want my two weeks' holiday too badly to take on any kind of job. Let that be clearly understood.'

'Two weeks' holiday!' exclaimed Reccivi. 'What could be more perfect!'

'I quite agree,' I said, firmly. 'Fourteen perfect days on the Devon coast, doing precisely nothing.'

'My dear Deane!' exclaimed Reccivi, obviously elated. 'Nothing could be better, as you will agree when I have told you what all this is about.' He finished his drink at a gulp, and stood up. 'There is nothing illegal about it, I assure you, nothing which an Englishman cannot do without the utmost freedom. Come, Deane, even if you refuse afterwards, it will do no harm to listen. It will not take half an hour.'

'Oh, all right,' I said, grudgingly, 'but you will be wasting your time.'

'It will be an enormous relief even to talk about it to a man of understanding,' said Reccivi, 'especially one who knows Italy and has an appreciation of beauty.' He glanced at a small Greuze, one of my few cherished possessions, but I was too dull-witted to understand why. 'You knew Arturo's, in Milan, did you not?'

'Of course,' I said.

'One of the most renowned galleries in Europe,' said Reccivi, and he was not exaggerating. 'I take especial pride in saying that, Deane, because I was one of the three partners in Arturo's. It was also an extremely wealthy concern; that will not surprise you?'

'No,' I said.

'I myself am wealthy,' said Reccivi. 'I lost a great deal during the war, but I am still rich. Unfortunately Arturo's was destroyed by fire after a bombing raid. It was a tragedy, one of the saddest things that could have happened. However, I was at all times a realist, Deane, and at heart a friend and admirer of the English. I could not believe that this country would be subjugated, and you will understand how deeply rooted was my belief when I tell you that I arranged for a large shipment of pictures and treasures to be brought to England *after* the war with Germany had begun and while Italy was still neutral. I cannot value the shipment, no man can. Every single thing included in it came from Arturo's and belonged to the company. Had the Axis partners won, I think Hitler would have turned on Italy with all the savagery with which he turned on other countries. Therefore, I believed that the goods were safer in England than in Italy. Not everything was brought here, of course, but a very large proportion of the company's stock. You understand?'

'Yes,' I said.

'When the galleries were burned down I congratulated myself more than ever upon the astuteness of my move,' said Reccivi, 'and I took pleasure in it for more reasons than one. My partners were less fortunate than I, for their personal fortunes were lost with Arturo's. Neither of them were enthusiastic Fascists and neither received any consideration when the Germans occupied northern Italy. They have now little more than the clothes they stand in and a roof over their heads. Charity they will not accept. They are proud, for they come from old Italian families, and—but you will understand that also,

16

I am sure, I tell you only that you may better understand what a tragedy it is.'

I said nothing, but his story gripped me.

'When the shipment was brought to England it was left in charge of an English dealer,' went on Reccivi. 'No money changed hands, but there was a private understanding that after the war Arturo's would recover the goods and pay a commission for their safe keeping. The dealer with whom I dealt was a man of irreproachable reputation. To satisfy your customs, it was declared that the goods were coming into the country for an exhibition. I do not know exactly how it was arranged, only that there were no difficulties. And . . .'

'The English dealer robbed you,' I said.

Reccivi looked at me intently.

'No, Deane. It was not quite so straightforward as that. If it were, then I would place the whole situation in the hands of your government, for I have nothing to hide. The dealer, of whom you may have heard, was Leonard Farring. Is the name familiar?'

'Yes,' I said.

I had never met Farring personally, but I knew his reputation, and had quite lately seen his name in the papers, though I could not remember the connection. As I returned Reccivi's gaze, I reflected that he had chosen his man well, for Farring, a wealthy philanthropist, was believed to be absolutely trustworthy.

'Then you will know how justified I was to trust him,' said Reccivi. 'I was successful in getting a message to him just after the armistice, and received an answer. Everything was intact and he told me that I had no cause at all to worry about the collection. I was delighted, although I had not seriously thought of any-

17

thing different. I will go as far as to admit that I obtained my present assignment so that I could come to England and see Farring. My chief objects were to arrange for a credit so that my partners in Italy would be in a happier position, and to arrange for the return of some of the collection so that business could start again. I reached England some weeks after Farring had gone into a nursing home for an operation—you heard about that, perhaps?'

'Of course, that was it!' I remembered what I had read about the art dealer immediately. 'A minor one, wasn't it?'

'So it said in the papers,' said Reccivi. 'I inquired at his home when he was expected back and was given vague replies. At first I put that down to the fact that I am Italian. Quite a number of my one-time English friends have cold-shouldered me, and I cannot be surprised at that.' He shrugged, and again I felt sorry for the man, although I was far more intrigued with his story, and eager for him to continue. He did so, in a quiet, careful voice. 'After a fortnight I began to press my enquiries. I still received only vague answers, so I obtained the address of the nursing home and inquired there. Farring left it two weeks ago, and I can find no trace of him!'

'Surely there's nothing remarkable in that,' I said. 'He may have gone into the country and given instructions that no one is to have his address. A lot of people do that when they are convalescing.'

'That is what one would think but for two things,' said Reccivi grimly. 'The first is that his daughter, Elizabeth, has no idea where he is, and the second . . .' Reccivi paused, then went on gravely: 'I was offered a small Corot by a Chelsea dealer with whom I did some business before the war, and I went to see it. Imagine my feelings when I discovered that it was a picture from the Arturo Collection.'

3

I Discuss the Matter Further

Although I suspected what was to follow when Reccivi mentioned the Corot, the statement shocked me. I did not question the truth of it. Perhaps I would not have been so affected but for the fact that in a modest way I myself am a collector. I have never had the money to buy what I would like, but now and again I have come across little masterpieces at a not-too-exorbitant figure; and these I treasure. The mystery naturally aroused my curiosity. It says much for the way in which Reccivi had told his story that I also felt sympathetic towards his two partners in Milan.

'Well, Deane?' he said, abruptly. 'Will you help me?'

'I don't see how I can,' I temporised.

'At the very least you can try to find out what has happened to Farring,' said Reccivi. 'I assure you that I am at least as concerned for him as I am for the collection. I cannot rid myself of the conviction that he is in some danger. His daughter's manner convinced me of that. She did not trust me, but it was abundantly clear that she is very much afraid. Yet if I try to find out more, on my own account, I will only meet with trouble from the authorities. If I take the story to the police or to the Home Office I might do something which will increase Farring's danger and his daughter's anxiety That is why I dare not take any action.'

'I see,' I said. 'What were you doing at the Chameleon?'

He shrugged. 'I was waiting for the dealer who offered me the Corot. I promised to meet him there at twelve o'clock. He did not arrive. I left the hotel and went to his shop.' Reccivi raised his hands in a helpless gesture. 'He was not there. I telephoned only an hour before I came to see you, but he had not returned. Perhaps I am wrong, but it seems to me that it is connected with the disappearance of Farring.'

'I don't think you ought to assume that Farring has disappeared,' I objected.

'It is impossible to do otherwise!' snapped Reccivi. 'If you will not help me, say so. There is no need to try to convince me that I am making a mystery where there is none!'

'Now don't get excited,' I said. 'I've already made my attitude clear. All I am trying to do is to show you that you may be taking too pessimistic a view. Of course,' I went on firmly, 'if Farring *has* been spirited away, and this Chelsea dealer is also missing, it's a disturbing situation, and one which must be handled by the police.'

'I was afraid that you might say that,' said Reccivi, 'but listen to me, Deane, please. I am convinced that Farring's daughter is *afraid* of going to the police. I said while I was with her that some inquiries should be made, but she immediately became alarmed. You see how helpless I am,' he added, despairingly. 'If I could find out where Farring has gone, if I could only make sure that there is some crime afoot, then I could do more. If St. Clare were here, I have little doubt that he would gladly help.'

'You probably misjudge him,' I said.

What he said about Cris was more than likely to be true, but I did not want to encourage Reccivi. If the facts were as bad as he imagined, it was a matter for the police, and if they were not, then the situation would resolve itself in time, without the need for anyone to work on it. Reccivi was naturally worked up and anxious; in such circumstances even the delay of a few days would seem unbearable, but I was able to take a more dispassionate view.

Yet as I looked into his face I had not the heart to refuse him. I read appeal there, and restraint because he had already asked more favours than he liked, and my attitude had piqued him and touched his pride.

At the back of my mind, of course, there was the possibility that he had not told the whole truth.

'So you can really do nothing,' he said, after a long pause.

'I don't think so,' I said, 'but if you care to let me sleep on it and tell me where I can get in touch with you tomorrow, I'll talk it over with my fiancée. Even if I can do nothing, I may be able to suggest something that will help.'

'You are very good,' said Reccivi.

He said that quietly, but he meant it, and I think he had obtained as much from me as he had expected. Looking back, I wonder why he attempted to get help from me. I think he was really desperate and, when he had glimpsed me at the hotel, had clutched at a straw. At least he had felt certain that I would not be prevented from helping because of risks.

I urged him to have another drink before he went, and this he did, expressing his thanks again and giving me his address. It appeared he was sleeping above the Gower Street offices, which had been set up for the repatriation work. I saw him out, and watched him disappear into the faint blue light.

He had given me plenty to think about, and taken up more time than I could well spare. I realised ruefully that I could not now catch the early-morning train on the morrow that I had hoped to do. I decided to telephone Sheila and give her an outline of what had happened.

When I replaced the receiver I was smiling to myself, and for the next few minutes I gave Reccivi very little thought. Then I finished off the reports, sealed them, heaved a sigh of relief, and locked them in my brief-case before going to bed.

I had just pulled on my pyjamas and was stubbing out a cigarette when I heard a scream.

I can't describe what I felt, but I knew at once that it was the beginning, a sign, of something that was to involve me deeply.

I reached for my dressing-gown, wrenched the door open, and hurried downstairs. Two men and a woman were on the landing below mine, and two other men in bath robes were coming up the stairs. Several people stood in the doorways of their flats. A man was bending over a figure on the ground, and I did not doubt for a moment that it was Reccivi.

He was on his side, with his eyes closed, and I saw the ugly wound at the side of his head.

The man straightened up as I reached him, and I asked abruptly:

'Is he alive?'

'Just about,' said the other. I recognised him as one of the tenants, although I knew none of the people very well who lived in the house.

'We'll have to get him into bed,' suggested someone.

'It's better not to move him,' I said. I had spent a year

as a medical student, and had a certain smattering of knowledge.

My words carried conviction. Someone telephoned for both a doctor and the police, while I stood by Reccivi, determined that no one else should get near him. I mentioned that he had been to visit me an hour before, and that seemed to break down the antagonism for which my abrupt manner was doubtless responsible.

The woman who had screamed was led away by her husband, and soon afterwards the doctor arrived. He was followed by a police sergeant who immediately telephoned for an ambulance, and then put in a call to his station. I was not surprised when police with cameras arrived.

I wanted no further proof of the gravity of Reccivi's discoveries about Farring, and I thought grimly that his desire to avoid sending for the police had been rudely shattered.

When the ambulance arrived most of the tenants retired. I was left with the man whom I had found bending over the body, and the police sergeant and two constables. They knew that Reccivi had been to see me, and I invited the sergeant upstairs.

By then, however, I had decided to tell him only the bare fact that Reccivi, an old acquaintance, had called to see me. There was just a chance that Clyde would be interested, and since Reccivi was an Italian the affair might come within his jurisdiction. Clyde was mostly concerned with Intelligence abroad, but was also liaison officer between the Foreign and Home Offices. It was obvious that the sergeant was curious, but when he saw my card of authority he professed to be satisfied and went off, after warning me that the Criminal Investigation Department would probably send someone to see me. I felt sure that he would leave a man outside my door, but that did not perturb me.

I was in a state of considerable confusion when I telephoned Clyde at his home; luckily he had not gone to bed. I told him just enough to make him decide to come round at once. I dressed again, thinking ruefully that the trip to Devon would probably have to be further postponed. I wondered how long Clyde would be, and was tempted to telephone Sheila again. Then I thought I heard a knock at the front door. I went to open it, but no one was there.

That's odd, I thought.

I closed the door, after making sure that there was not even a policeman in sight, and turned round. As I did so I caught sight of a man standing in the doorway of the living-room. He was covering me with an automatic.

4

I Need No Further Convincing

Keeping the automatic trained on me, the intruder walked to the hall door and shot the bolt.

I watched him closely, storing up the details of his face for future reference. He was heavily disguised with cheek-pads, false eyebrows and moustache.

'Go into that room,' he said, motioning to the dining-room.

'Not being a spirit as yet, I can hardly walk through a locked door,' I said drily.

'Where is the key?'

'In my bedroom.'

'Walk to it, keeping close to the wall.'

There was nothing unusual about the voice, except that it was that of an educated man. I obeyed him until I stood with my back to the bedroom door, which was ajar. I thought I might get a chance of backing quickly into the room and closing the door before he could follow, but this hope was doomed at once.

'Kick the door open,' he said, 'and walk backwards to the chair by the bed.'

I obeyed, thinking that he meant to give me no chance to pick up the chair and use it as a weapon. I was now beyond the reach of any missile except a pillow, and I would have to turn round to get at that. He stood near the door, so motionless that I began to feel really anxious; there was something sinister about his manner, something ruthless about the way he gave orders. I knew that Clyde would arrive before long, but did not know whether to be glad or sorry. If we were interrupted before this man had finished what he wanted to do, he might shoot me.

'I have some questions to ask you, and I expect prompt replies.' That was all he said by way of preamble, as if he knew that the gun was a sufficient threat. 'Why did Reccivi come to see you?'

'We are old acquaintances,' I said.

'I said *why*.'

'That is why,' I told him.

'What reason did he give?' He sounded impatient.

'He told me that he had seen me at the Chameleon this morning, and decided to call on me as soon as he could.'

The man said sharply: 'You are wasting time!'

'I can't do more than answer your questions,' I retorted. I knew that at all costs I must not tell him all that Reccivi had said to me, although I would have to give him a more satisfactory explanation of his visit than I had done so far. The important thing was to make him think that I was scared—which was not difficult!—and also that I was telling the truth.

'Reccivi didn't call on you so late at night just to renew an old acquaintance,' said the stranger.

'I agree with you,' I said slowly. The response seemed to startle him.

'What do you mean?'

'I got the impression that he wanted to ask or tell me something, and couldn't screw up enough courage to do it,' I said. 'He kept leading up to it, but never quite got there. I've some idea of what it was about, now.'

'What do you mean?' he repeated, more sharply.

'Before he left the house he was savagely attacked, and I think he is dead,' I said, deliberately, and I was rewarded. A look of relief spread over the man's face. When he spoke next I was not unduly perturbed. His voice was harsher, but I knew it was only to impress me.

'I think you're lying. Reccivi came here to ask you to help him!'

'It wouldn't surprise me,' I said. 'He hinted at having enemies in England and that it was pleasant to feel that he had friends here, in case he needed to get in touch with them, but he didn't go any further.'

'Didn't you ask him to explain?'

'I did not,' I said. 'Earlier in the day when I saw him in England I reported it to the authorities. I needn't have worried, as he appears to have every right to be here. We were acquaintances before the war, but I have no wish to further the acquaintanceship, and I think I made that quite clear to him.' I drew in a deep breath.

'If you want to know what Reccivi came for, *I* can't tell you—but I can tell you one or two things.'

'Go on,' he said.

'I telephoned a friend as soon as I knew that Reccivi was hurt, and I have been threatened with another visit from the police. Both my friend and the police are likely to arrive here at any time, and the front of the house is watched. You came in through the back door, didn't you?'

'What are you driving at?' he asked. I had worried him, which was some reason for satisfaction.

'Another thing I can tell you is that neighbours heard Reccivi and the quarrelling,' I said, 'and the police will know about that. I think they will make sure that I can't get out either way, and a watch will soon be put on the back door if it has not been done already.'

'What did you quarrel about?' he demanded, and I had to admire the cool way in which he ignored my implications.

I shrugged my shoulders.

'He was only allowed to bring a little money into the country, and he wanted to borrow some. When I refused he lost his temper.'

Not once in the course of the interview had the man removed his gaze from my face. There was a pause, while he tried to make up his mind, and then he spoke abruptly.

'I hope you haven't lied to me, Deane.' He moved to one side, pulling the door open. 'Go into the kitchen.'

It was an uncomfortable feeling walking with my back towards him, but I thought I knew what he was going to do; if I was right, he would not shoot me.

'Open the back door,' he said.

I obeyed, and as I did so the light went out and was replaced by a torch.

'Go down quietly, Deane. If you make too much noise, or try to run away, I shall shoot you.'

I did not answer, but went down the iron staircase cautiously. If a policeman was watching, I would walk into him, and the gunman would slip away before the man realised that two people had come down the stairs. I imagined him keeping close to the wall, where it was darkest, leaving me clearly visible in the moonlight.

As I expected, so it happened. As I reached the last step a policeman stepped out of the shadows.

'Good evening, sir.'

I had no time to admire that disarming greeting for as I drew close to the policeman I muttered:

'There's an armed man behind me. Be careful!'

Then I swung round.

I was in time to see the man swinging himself over the railings of the staircase. He dropped lightly to the ground, and began to run. I gave chase and the policeman was quick-witted enough, for I had hardly gone a dozen steps before the blast of his whistle broke the quiet.

I raced along, fairly sure that the man would not risk the time to turn and shoot me. The corner was the danger spot, but this, too, I engineered without mishap.

I caught sight of the fugitive racing towards Clarges Street. A helmeted policeman tried to head him off, and I yelled out a warning that the man was armed.

The warning appeared to come too late, for the policeman reeled back as the fugitive plunged into the network of narrow streets that bordered the West End.

The policeman who had blown his whistle touched my arm.

'You'd better leave it to us, sir.'

He escorted me to the front door of the flat, and there I lost all interest in him and his companions, for on the doorstep was Sheila. I took her arm, and guided her up the stairs, only to realise when I got there that the front door was bolted. As I drew my hand away from my pocket, Sheila said:

'Don't say you've forgotten your keys!'

'As a matter of fact, I have,' I said, 'but this time it's bolted.'

'*Now* what have you been up to?'

I recognised the deep voice of Sir Alan Clyde, and turned to welcome him. I explained the predicament, and we went downstairs together and conferred with the constable, who escorted us to the back door. Not until we were inside did he leave us, with another courtly good night.

I led the others into the sitting-room, then told them exactly what had happened, repeating Reccivi's story and the conversation with the gunman as literally as I could.

All the time I was doing so Clyde's grey eyes, deepset beneath prominent eyebrows, did not glance away from me. He is a well-built man of medium height, immaculately dressed on all occasions. I have already said that he is a liaison officer, but he is also many other things. If the Foreign Office wants an unusual job handled discreetly and well, Clyde usually gets it. Crispian St. Clare, Anton Duval and I are always responsible to Clyde, but whether he is also the head of other sections of the Intelligence Department, I really don't know, although I have worked for him for years.

Both of them heard me out in silence.

'And that's all I can tell you,' I said.

'It doesn't seem to come under my jurisdiction,' said Clyde, 'unless . . .' He paused.

'Unless Reccivi is really spying in England,' said Sheila.

'That's a bit far-fetched,' I objected.

'It's a possibility,' said Clyde, 'although I'm inclined to think that he was telling the truth. What do you think about it, Ned?'

I looked at Sheila.

'If it's a police matter, I don't see that it need affect us.'

'We might hold a watching brief,' suggested Clyde, scratching his chin reflectively. 'What do you think, Sheila? It would interfere with your plans, but . . .' He broke off.

'Look here, do you want us to hold a watching brief?' I demanded bluntly.

My feelings were mixed, and in fact I was largely influenced by what Sheila thought. By that time my dreams of a quiet holiday in Devon had faded, and at the back of my mind I knew that even if we got away, I would be preoccupied, wondering what was happening to Farring and his daughter, and the Chelsea art dealer who also seemed to have mysteriously disappeared.

'I don't know that I do,' said Clyde, 'and even if I did I would, in ordinary circumstances, pass it on to someone else. As it is, through no design of our own, you've been pitched into this, Ned, and you might not be able to get out of it even if you want to. If they've taken the trouble to visit you once, they might do so again.'

'Now you're getting fanciful,' I said. I smiled at Sheila. 'Plans as arranged, I think, don't you?'

30

Sheila shook her head.

'I doubt very much if that's possible.' She looked at Clyde. 'Alan, do you think we could help?'

The 'we' took me off guard, and I was about to protest when Clyde said that it was a confused business and the best thing we could do was to go to bed, and hope that something was settled by the morning. He promised to see to the police so that I need not be bothered again that night, and went off, leaving Sheila and I sitting opposite each other in easy chairs, waiting for the other to speak.

'Well . . .'

'What . . .' began Sheila, almost simultaneously.

'It's a hopeless mix-up!' I declared.

'And I'm going to make it worse,' said Sheila quietly, 'for I know Elizabeth Farring.'

5

In Which Plans are Altered

Sheila had known Farring's daughter for some years. They were not close friends, but were members of one or two charity organisations. Elizabeth acted for her father, Sheila told me, and often had substantial funds at her disposal. She had only met Leonard Farring once or twice but had been very favourably impressed, and it was apparent that she thought highly of Elizabeth.

I had been puzzled by her attitude when Clyde had been at the flat; now I knew what caused it. If it were true that Elizabeth Farring was in trouble, she would like to help. She had noticed that Elizabeth had been preoccupied recently, and several acquaintances had also observed it.

'That rather bears out what Reccivi said,' Sheila declared. 'Look here, Ned, you're the judge, you know whether you feel fit enough to help if you should be asked, or whether you really need a good rest.'

I smiled. 'I can manage, if needs be, and I'll gladly help if I can, but I don't see that I can do much.'

'You always underrate yourself,' said Sheila. 'Reccivi didn't come to you because he happens to know you, but because he knew that if you would rise to the bait you would make a better job of it than most.'

'Oh, stuff and nonsense!' I said.

'Neither one nor the other,' said Sheila calmly, 'but let's wait until the morning, and see what the police say. I can't believe that if there is a mystery about Farring's disappearance they won't know something about it. I wonder why Reccivi was attacked,' she added musingly.

'I'd like to know that, too.'

That was the trouble: questions kept cropping up and would continue to do so, wherever we were. I knew it, and I had little doubt that our plans would have to be changed, although I had no notion of how the change would come about.

I saw Sheila back to her flat, and the moonlit streets reminded me that I did not know whether the man who had threatened me had been caught. I did not know whether Reccivi were alive, either. When I got back to Clarges Street I felt that I would not be able to settle to sleep until I knew about Reccivi, so I telephoned Bow Street. There was some delay before I was told that he was alive but on the danger list. They would not tell me in which hospital he was. When I asked whether they had captured the other man, I was answered with an evasive: 'Not as far as I know, sir,' which suggested that he was still at large.

In bed, the many confusing features of the affair kept running through my mind. It seemed likely that Reccivi had pressed his inquiries about Farring too far, and been attacked because of that; if it were so, there was no possible doubt that Farring was in grave danger. When I reached that point I began to argue with myself; nothing was yet clear enough for definite theories. The only established facts were that Reccivi had come to ask for my help, had been watched and attacked, and I had been visited to find out whether he had told me anything of importance.

There was some satisfaction in having bluffed the gunman, and with that thought I fell asleep.

I slept late, and by nine o'clock I had had three telephone calls. The first was from Sheila, who wanted to reassure herself that I was all right, the second was from Clyde, to say that a superintendent from Scotland Yard, named Webb, was coming to see me during the morning, and the third was from a sergeant who made an appointment for Webb to call at half past ten. I immediately telephoned Sheila, whom I thought would like to be present at the interview. Instead, she hesitated.

'What else are you going to do?' I demanded, suspiciously.

'I thought I would see Elizabeth Farring,' said Sheila, 'I won't tell her anything . . .'

'Much,' I interrupted.

'Well, there's no law against seeing her, is there?' demanded Sheila, 'and it affects her as much as it does anyone.'

'You may be right,' I said. 'Will you promise to come straight here afterwards?'

'If you'll stay there, yes.'

'I won't leave until you've arrived,' I promised her.

I went downstairs where the caretakers in the basement flat ran a restaurant for the tenants. The room was crowded. I had to wait ten minutes for a table, and was aware of many curious glances.

There was a brief mention of Reccivi's 'accident' in most of the morning papers, although no details were given and no names were mentioned. I was relieved about that, but not surprised when I got upstairs and found two strangers waiting outside the door. They were newspapermen. I pretended to be frank with them, admitted that Reccivi had visited me but the rest was a complete mystery. Then one of them startled me by asking:

'Was it Count Leonardo Reccivi, Mr. Deane?'

'Yes—an old acquaintance,' I said brightly.

'Didn't he once sentence you to death?'

I stared at him, and then managed to compose myself enough to smile.

'He did. How on earth did you get hold of that information?'

'We see a lot of news that we can't publish,' the man said. 'You're sure there's nothing else for us, Mr. Deane?'

'You're a sceptical fellow, aren't you?' I said. 'All I can tell you is that Superintendent Webb is coming to see me during the morning, and presumably he will be handling the case.'

'Webb on it, is he!' exclaimed the other reporter. 'You're in high society!'

They did not ask further questions, but I doubted whether they would be far away when the superintendent arrived. Their manner had aroused my curiosity about Webb, and I awaited his arrival with interest. He turned out to be a massive, slow-moving man with heavy-lidded eyes.

'You didn't have a very nice experience last night, Mr. Deane, I'm told.'

'I've had worse,' I said.

'So I have heard!'

'Is Reccivi still alive?'

'I think we shall pull him through,' Webb assured me comfortably. 'He looked worse than he was, but they meant to murder him all right.'

'Did you get the other man?'

'I wish we had,' said Webb, fervently, 'I really wish we had! Among the things I'd like you to do is write out his description as clearly as you can.'

'It won't help much,' I said, and told him why. He nodded portentously; I began to feel impatient, and asked bluntly: 'Did you know that there was any trouble before yesterday?'

'Not with Reccivi,' said Webb, 'but we had an idea that things were not very well with Farring. There was not much we could do about it. His daughter would make no complaint, and as much as told us to mind our own business. Nothing has been reported lost, stolen or strayed.' A faint gleam appeared in Webb's eyes. 'Even what happened last night doesn't give us any justification for inquiring too closely into Farring's whereabouts. All we know is that Count Reccivi wanted to see him and was told that he was not available. Did you know that he was a partner in this Italian firm?'

'Not before he told me so,' I said.

'Well, there you are,' said Webb. 'He would have to supply evidence of ownership, evidence that the goods were put in Farring's charge, evidence that he has been refused access to them. That's not to mention the fact

35

that it raises a ticklish problem, because Farring should not have received these goods as a custodian. You say Reccivi says that the politer formalities were observed?'

'He did,' I said.

'I'll check up on that,' said Webb. 'Well now, where are we?' I got the impression that he was mildly amused for some obscure reason. 'We are at the point where we know that a crime was committed against Reccivi's person and that your flat was burglariously entered and that you were threatened with bodily violence. Our job is to find out who did those things, as we shall, Mr. Deane, have no doubt of that!'

'The police always get their man,' I quoted, drily.

'That's truer than you might think,' said Webb, good-humouredly. 'And now, Mr. Deane, I have a confession to make. I have been making inquiries about you and your friends. Sir Alan Clyde was good enough to give me some remarkable information about you. Fascinating business,' he added, unexpectedly, 'I wouldn't have thought you had it in you!'

'Indeed?' I said.

'No offence intended, Mr. Deane! I wouldn't have thought *any* man had it in him to go in and out of France and Italy and to do the things you've done— but that hardly affects the present case, you think. That's where you're wrong, sir, it does affect it. Mr. Deane, I will put my cards on the table. I can assert no authority, apply no compulsion, offer you no reward, guarantee you no danger. As for the first three things, how I wish I could!'

'Supposing you get to the point?' I suggested.

'Well, here it is,' said Webb with a great show of frankness. 'Your fiancée is a friend of Elizabeth Farring. At the moment I have no authority to inquire into the whereabouts of Farring himself, but I want to know where he is. I want to make sure that he is in good health and in no danger. I don't say that I could not call upon some obscure regulation and obtain the necessary authority, but I doubt whether it would be wise. My information is that whenever Farring's daughter or other close acquaintances of Farring are questioned by the police, they become evasive. *Now*, Mr. Deane, a friend of Miss Farring's might have better luck, don't you think?'

'In other words, you want me to make inquiries into Farring's so-called disappearance,' I said.

'That's it in a nutshell,' declared Superintendent Webb. 'In a nutshell, Mr. Deane. I can offer you the support of the police wherever you may find yourself, subject to your providing the evidence that the circumstances prevailing need the presence of the police. I shall *not* want it known that you are assisting us in any way, naturally. In fact . . .' He broke off, smiling slightly.

'Go on,' I said.

'In fact,' repeated Webb, 'I would like it to appear as if you have some personal motive. A desire for reward, shall we say. You know Reccivi's story. You may be justified in thinking that if you find these art treasures the firm of Arturo's might be expected to recompense you handsomely. That would be much more satisfactory than admitting a desire for adventure. The number of men who throw themselves into danger for the sake of adventure is remarkably small.'

'Is this an official proposition?' I demanded.

'It is and it isn't,' said Webb. 'I carry no written instructions. It is not a suggestion which I would put to any man who did not have the reputation and the official approval which you possess. It is unorthodox, and unorthodoxy is looked upon with horror at Scotland Yard; and yet I assure you that no difficulties in which you might find yourself would be considered your responsibility. If you care to speak to Sir Alan, he will confirm that this suggestion is being made to you with his approval, and that is not a thing he gives lightly.'

That finally settled the matter.

'All right,' I said.

Webb stood up ponderously.

'Well, well, Mr. Deane, I will not conceal from you that that is a great relief, a very great relief. After you have seen Miss Farring, what do you propose to do?'

'A word with the art dealer who tried to sell the Corot picture to Reccivi wouldn't do any harm,' I said. 'Have you found him?'

He looked at me for a moment, his eyes alert in the folds of his massive face. When he spoke, his voice was without expression.

'Yes, we have. He has been murdered.'

6

A Talk with Elizabeth

I don't know why this latest development affected me so much. I knew that Reccivi had come within an ace of being murdered, and I had been convinced that if I made a false move, the man would have killed me the previous night, but now, for the first time, horror touched me.

Webb had little to say about it.

The dealer, a man named Forbes, had been found in the well of the lift at the block of flats where he lived. The head injuries were not unlike those inflicted on Reccivi, but it was not certain that the same instrument had been used. The police were searching his flat and his shop premises for the Corot, or any further items from the Arturo Collection, but nothing had yet been found.

Webb did not advance any theory. The only one that seemed to answer was that Forbes had been killed because of the Corot. He had a sound reputation, and doubtless he would have told the police where he obtained it; someone had made that impossible.

I was able to get a taxi for Regent's Park and the address which Sheila had given me, but we were held up by innumerable traffic blocks, and the journey seemed never ending. The frequent stopping and starting prevented me from concentrating on all that happened, and I alternated between moments of acute depression and unjustifiable optimism.

I have never had much to do with Scotland Yard, though I knew a little of its enormous activities and the thoroughness with which it worked. It was Webb's vagueness and the fact that so powerful an authority felt it necessary to appeal to me to find out what they had failed to do, which affected me so much. Working in England on such an affair as this would be very different from working in Europe with the Germans in occupation, and I was a long way from convinced that I had the qualifications for the job.

Then I asked myself what 'such a job as this' really meant. Was the Arturo Collection missing? Had Farring been kidnapped and was he being held to ransom? I thought this possible, and it would explain his daughter's anxiety and the reluctance of his friends to discuss the matter with the police. That might also explain why Webb had come to me; he might suspect such a crime but be unable to prove it.

By the time the taxi turned into Warren Terrace another thing had established itself firmly in my mind. The major difference between working here and in Europe was that Cris and Anton were not at hand. I had come to rely on Cris for instructions; with him, I had only occasionally worked on my own initiative. At heart, I think I was afraid because I might fail in a crisis at a time when Sheila was dependent on me.

The taxi stopped, and cut across my reflections.

Farring's house in Warren Street was tall and narrow. There was a short flight of steps to the front door, the brasses of which caught the sun and shot golden rays in many directions.

An old manservant admitted me, saying that I was expected. As he flung open a door, Sheila turned from the window, while Elizabeth Farring rose from a chair by the fireplace.

She made an instant impression on me.

She was tall, and she struck me as being a mannish, confident, perhaps aggressive woman. She was older than I had expected, perhaps thirty-two or three. Her features were well-cut with the precision one expects in a sculpture, her hair a glorious auburn.

I had been prepared to meet a timid and anxious girl who would turn to me eagerly for help, and this bronzed Amazon astonished me.

She gave my hand a grip that was painfully firm.

'I thought you were never coming.'

'I came as quickly as I could,' I said.

'I still can't make up my mind whether to be glad or sorry that you are taking an interest in this affair.' Her voice was powerful but pleasant. 'Why you and Sheila should pitch yourselves into danger for my sake

I don't know,' she went on. 'I'm not sure that I shall let you.'

'Danger?' I said, mildly.

'You don't imagine that it's not dangerous, do you?' demanded Elizabeth. 'You don't think I've been scared out of my wits for months for nothing?' She moved about the room restlessly. 'If you want any convincing that it is dangerous, I can do it. Reccivi told you about Forbes, didn't he?'

'The Chelsea dealer who . . .'

'The Chelsea dealer who tried to sell him a piece of his own collection,' snapped Elizabeth. 'Well, Forbes has been *murdered*!'

I was surprised that she knew this.

'Yes, *murdered*,' she repeated, grimly. 'I don't know why, I don't know anything, except that before he went into the nursing home my father was as frightened as I am now, although he wouldn't admit it, and wouldn't tell me a thing. When he didn't come home again . . .'

She broke off, staring out into the narrow, attractive garden for several minutes, her body rigid.

Sheila broke the silence.

'Elizabeth has told me about it,' she said, 'and Reccivi is right, Ned. No one knows where Mr. Farring is.'

Elizabeth swung round.

'I haven't known where to find him for six weeks, and it seems like an eternity! I don't know what is happening to him, I can't even be sure that he is alive.'

I said: 'Then why haven't you been to the police?'

'Police, police!' echoed Elizabeth fiercely. 'All people can do is to prattle about the police! I haven't been to them because I've been told not to!'

'Told?' I repeated.

'Yes, told in plain words that if I do I shall not see

41

him again. If they had only asked for money it would not have mattered, I would have paid them whatever they asked. But all they demand is that I shall keep silent. What they will do when they know that I've talked to you . . .'

But she told me very little more than I already knew. There had been some mystery about her father before his illness. The operation had been successful and he had been planning to go to the West Country for a month's convalescence. Elizabeth had made the arrangements for a car to fetch him, and gone with it, only to find that he had already been taken from the nursing home. Knowing that there was some mystery going on, she had accepted this without comment, returning to Warren Terrace, beside herself with anxiety. Within an hour she had received a telephone message, purporting to come from her father, saying that he was quite safe and would get in touch with her shortly. In the three weeks which had followed she had received three letters, all of them written by him, all in the same strain; he was all right and she was not to worry.

Then Reccivi came to see her, and she put him off, knowing that she did not sound very convincing. It was almost immediately after his visit that a man called on her after dark. All she knew about him was that he wore an absurd false moustache and eyebrows. He had warned her that she must not go to the police if she wanted her father to return alive, and the same man—at least she thought it was the same voice—had warned her on the telephone several times since.

I made no comment during this recital, and gave no sign that I recognised the description of the man who had warned her. By the time she had finished, however, I saw no point in hiding the fact that he had also visited me. She would probably find out that Reccivi had been injured and suspect that the police had questioned me. All the same, I said nothing of that, but told her more about Reccivi's visit. Of the man with the gun, I merely said that I had convinced him that Reccivi had given me no details, and that he had gone away, presumably satisfied.

'So that is why you were so anxious to come and see me,' Elizabeth said, looking at Sheila. 'Why didn't you go to the police?'

Evasion would be no use; I had to tell a direct lie, or else the truth. Of the two, the truth saves a great many complications and needless difficulties, and I foresaw difficulties enough with Elizabeth Farring. I weighed it all up quickly, and then I told her exactly what had happened and what Webb wanted me to do.

The colour ebbed from her cheeks. I knew that Sheila thought that I was making a mistake.

When I had finished the story, I said gently:

'If we are going to work together, you must know exactly how much I've been told and what I am supposed to be doing; but there is no need for me to tell others exactly what transpires.'

'What do you mean?' she demanded.

'I am not a policeman,' I reminded her, 'but a private citizen with certain advantages. It's obvious that if these people suspect that I am working for the police they may do harm to your father, but they can only find that out if I resort to the police. Webb made it clear that I need not do so unless I wanted to. Webb is prepared to rely on my sense of propriety to tell him if I discover anything illegal, but he wouldn't tie himself down to making my appointment official, and so I am not obliged to keep the police advised of what happens. Therefore, the johnny who fancies himself in disguise can think that I am only taking a private interest. In fact if we get in touch with him we can let him believe that I think there might be profit in it, to explain my interest.'

'It would never work,' she said. 'You would run to the police about the slightest thing.'

'I've been used to working without consulting any authorities,' I said stiffly.

'Sheila has told me what you do.'

'Then you might have the sense to realise that if I can spend weeks together abroad, keeping away from the authorities, I can manage it in England, where my papers are all in order. Look here, Elizabeth, I would like to help. I know your father's reputation and I like Reccivi and would also be glad to help him. On the other hand I don't propose to do anything if you are going to be hostile, or decide to keep back relevant facts.'

'What do you mean by that?' she demanded, sharply.

'It's simple enough,' I said. 'You're probably afraid of what the expert in disguise will do if he finds out that I have the confidence of the police; but you've another reason for being anxious to avoid them, haven't you?'

That stung her. I wondered if she were going to refuse to admit it, but she said:

'How did you guess?'

'Your manner made it pretty obvious.'

She looked at me sharply, and a little shamefaced.

'I suppose you have to know everything now, little though it is. Yes, I am afraid of what the police might find out, I am afraid of what *I* might find out. I discovered some time ago, soon after I knew that my father was being harassed, that some of the Arturo Collection had been sold, and the money credited to my father's account. I think that someone found out that my father was selling goods which did not belong to him, and I am afraid that he is being blackmailed. I suppose I am all kinds of a damned fool to tell you,' she added, bitterly. 'Now you've probably discovered what Webb asked you to, and you'll go running to him with the whole story. If you do . . .'

She broke off, as if she realised that I could do so, and there was no way in which she could prevent it.

7

I am Further Puzzled by the Police

I managed to convince her that I did not intend to act as an *agent provocateur* for the police, and that I was genuinely anxious to help her to find her father. She wanted to believe it, which made the task easier. Before we could go further into it, a maid came in to ask whether Sheila and I would be staying to lunch.

'Yes,' said Elizabeth, 'will you . . . ?'

'I think it would be a good idea if we all went out together,' I said.

When the maid had gone I pointed out that the house was probably being watched, and that both Sheila and I had been seen. There was no point in staying in or trying to make it look as if we wanted to conceal the fact that we had visited Warren Terrace. I telephoned for a table at the Chameleon, Elizabeth going upstairs to change, taking Sheila with her.

That done, I went to the front door and let myself out.

I was convinced that the house was being watched, and wanted to see anyone who might be in sight. The park was an excellent place, of course; anyone could lounge there indefinitely. There were several people lying on the grass, several others on wooden benches. I strolled across the road idly, and as if without purpose. I have a good memory for faces, and I knew that I would not forget any face I saw. I picked out no one who had any sinister look about him. The most striking fellow was an old tramp with aquiline features and curly white hair. He was lying on his back, with his hands clasped behind his head. A nurse and two small children passed me.

I went back to the house, standing beside a window, hoping that one of the people I had noticed would show some interest; but I had no luck.

It was an uncomfortable feeling that in some way we were dependent on what move the other side made. I went over in my mind all that Elizabeth had told me. It did not amount to much, only to the fact that she appeared to believe her father might have taken the pieces and sold them. It was possible she was right, although it seemed quite out of character.

At half past twelve the girls came downstairs, Elizabeth dressed rather magnificently in a sable-trimmed coat.

She was well known at the Chameleon, and I wished I had chosen some place where she would have been less conspicuous. But she seemed to enjoy it, talking vivaciously, a febrile excitement overruling her fears.

It was two o'clock before we left the dining-room and went into the lounge for coffee. The waiter who served us returned a few minutes afterwards, and I thought he had the bill. Instead, he slipped a piece of folded paper into my hand, murmuring:

'A gentleman gave me this, sir, and asked me to pass it on.'

'Oh,' I said. 'Which gentleman?'

The waiter looked round, but said that the man had gone. I opened the note. In pencilled capital letters were the words: *So you are a liar, Mr. Deane.*

There was nothing else. I handed it to the others, without speaking. Elizabeth's colour heightened, and she said quickly: 'Are you sure you're wise to go on with it?'

'I'm not worried by surreptitious notes,' I said. 'I think we have got them guessing, and you'll almost certainly have a visitor this afternoon, but I doubt whether he will try to do anything.'

I was less confident than I sounded, and wished it were possible to stop Sheila from going back with Elizabeth. She would refuse of course. The danger was there and she would insist on facing it. I hailed a taxi for them, saw them into it, and walked briskly towards Clarges Street. But I had a most uncomfortable feeling that I was being followed.

I half-expected to find someone waiting for me at the flat, but no one was there. I wished heartily that Cris and Anton were in England. Reccivi was right: both of them would jump at the chance of playing some part in this business, although I doubted whether they would be back for a week.

By that time I hoped fervently it woud be over.

The telephone bell made me start. I picked up the receiver, thinking it might be the sender of the message, my heart beating fast. Instead, Superintendent Webb's deep, slow voice came on the line.

'Good afternoon, Mr. Deane. How are you progressing?'

'Fairly well,' I said, cautiously.

'I understand that you have taken Miss Farring out

to lunch,' said Webb, with a chuckle. 'That suggests that you are in the lady's favour—congratulations!'

'Thanks,' I said, drily.

'I hope you won't imagine that I telephoned to tell you that,' said Webb, 'I simply mentioned it in passing. I . . .'

'Now I'll mention something in passing,' I said. 'If you expect me to get the best out of this business, don't have me followed. For one reason, I might think it is someone in the enemy's camp, and get violent.'

Webb chuckled again.

'No need for truculence, Mr. Deane. As a matter of fact I thought it would be a very useful thing if you were followed by one of my men. There's more than a chance you might also be followed by someone in the enemy's camp, as you so aptly put it, and in that case he would immediately come to the conclusion that I was suspicious of you!'

'Well, yes,' I admitted reluctantly.

'I'm glad you approve,' said Webb. 'I still haven't come to the real reason for this call, though. I have an item of news which I think might interest you. I have had a report from the village of Menlow that Mr. Farring has been seen there.'

'Menlow, near Salisbury?' I demanded.

'Yes, that's the place. It's only a report, and it could be a case of mistaken identity, but I thought you would be interested. If you can go down to Menlow, it might be an advantage.'

I forebore to ask him why he did not send one of his own men down there if, as was apparent, he had thought it wise to put out a country-wide call for reports on Farring. It looked to me as if Webb had not told me all he knew.

I looked up the trains to Salisbury. There was one from Waterloo at five o'clock and another at seven-thirty-five. The A.A. book told me that there were only two hotels in the village, and I telephoned the larger, only to find that there was no accommodation. The smaller one was able to offer me a double and a single room, and I booked them for the next three nights and said that I would tell them on the next day whether I wanted to stay longer.

I was glad that something had turned up, but I was very much on edge. The odd thing was that I wanted the man who was so fond of disguise to come and see me, but I waited in vain. Then I began to worry in case Sheila and Elizabeth had been lured from the house, and at half past four I could contain myself no longer.

Nothing had happened at Regent's Park.

'So one trick hasn't worked,' I said to Sheila. 'And now for another plan. Can you and Elizabeth pack for at least a night and catch the seven-thirty-five train to Salisbury?'

'Yes, but why?' asked Sheila, quickly.

'The police think we might find something of interest down there,' I said, and then added: 'Now keep this to yourself, and don't tell Elizabeth. Farring is reported to have been seen at Menlow. We don't want to raise Elizabeth's hopes, so we'll just tell her that they've tipped me off to go down there. Is that all clear?'

We chatted on for a few minutes, and then rang off.

I went into my bedroom, loaded an automatic pistol, slipping two extra clips into my suitcase, and then began to pack.

.   .   .   .   .

It was after ten o'clock when we reached the village. The hotel, a small country inn which appeared to have little to commend it, could not or would not find us anything more than a pot of stewed tea and some biscuits. We ate and drank in a cold lounge over which the smell of stale beer and tobacco hung unpleasantly. The journey had been wearisome and we retired soon afterwards.

Our rooms turned out to be more comfortable than they looked, and after a good night we were down to breakfast by half past eight.

'It isn't going to be so bad, after all,' I said.

'Didn't Webb give you any idea why he suggested us coming?' asked Elizabeth.

'No, he was pretty vague, as he has been about the whole business. I shouldn't worry about that. We don't intend to take him into our confidence any more than he does us.'

'I am just beginning to believe that I can really trust you,' admitted Elizabeth.

The words pleased me. A good night's sleep was partly responsible, of course, but she was a woman whose approval and liking it was pleasant to have. All the same, I reflected a little sadly, it hardly made up for not being here alone with Sheila.

A waiter brought me the bill.

I looked at it in surprise.

'There's some mistake, I think. We shall be staying for several nights.'

The waiter shook his head.

'We're booked up after today for several weeks, sir, but I'll make enquiries.'

He let us staring at each other in bewilderment. He was away some time. At last I grew tired of waiting and walked towards the office. The door was not shut, and a low-pitched, querulous voice was perfectly audible to me.

'I don't care what they say, we've got to get them out of here.'

'He won't like it.'

'Go and tell him it was a mistake, we could only take them for one night!' ordered the querulous voice. There was a new note in it, one, if I was not greatly mistaken, of fear.

I went along, as if I had heard nothing.

Through the open window-hatch I saw the waiter, standing indecisively, and an old man sitting at a littered roll-top desk. His grey hair wanted cutting and his straggly moustache was stained yellow in the centre. When he saw me he jumped up from his chair, his whole attitude one of barely concealed terror.

8

We Seek New Quarters

I pretended to accept the situation with good grace, and the old man was garrulous with apologies. I told the others that he was not likely to change his mind, and agreed with them that someone had obviously coerced him into giving us notice.

I was rather pleased; it meant that that someone wanted to get us out of Menlow.

Shelia and Elizabeth went to the other hotel in the village to make inquiries, while I waited for the old man to leave the office. When he did so I followed him. I saw the door into which he went, and would have gone in after him had I not heard the sound of a telephone receiver being lifted.

As I gently pushed the door ajar, I heard him give a number. Footsteps were echoing upstairs and downstairs in the hotel, and I was afraid that before he started to speak I would be seen.

'Hallo,' said the old man. 'Hallo! Is that ... ?'

He gave no name, but seemed satisfied, and after another short pause he said:

'Yes, they're going. He didn't like it, but he didn't raise much trouble ... Yes, today ... That's all very well, but what about my business?'

He spoke in an aggrieved tone, yet the note of fear remained. There was further desultory conversation, and finally he rang off.

I slipped into the girls' room and waited for the old man to return to the office. When I heard his step on the stairs I crept back and tried the door. It was locked.

I whipped out my penknife, a tool of many purposes, and started to pick the lock. It was an old-fashioned one and took me less than a minute. As I opened the door I heard footsteps in the passage. Looking round, I saw one of the hotel residents, a middle-aged woman with elaborately dressed hair, walking briskly towards me.

She murmured a conventional greeting to which I replied, suppressing a temptation to enlarge on the weather. There is always, on these occasions, in one's relief at not being caught out, an urge to overplay one's hand.

I waited until she was halfway down the stairs and then slipped into the room. I closed the door behind me and lifted the telephone receiver.

'I had a call put in to London fifteen minutes ago,' I said, 'can you tell me how long it will be, please?'

'Just a moment, sir, I'll give you trunks.'

Trunks' supervisor assured me that no call had been put in to London that morning; in fact there had been no long-distance call, she said. That was something. I recalled the local exchange, and complained that the trunks operator seemed to have forgotten me; was it possible that a London call had been put through from the village?'

'No, sir,' said the girl, 'as a matter of fact there's only been one call from your number this morning, and that was to a Menlow number.'

'That's astonishing,' I said, and then, as if I had an inspiration: 'Was it Menlow 23?'

'No—Menlow 101, sir.'

I was well satisfied when I replaced the receiver. It should not be difficult to find out the name of the subscriber to Menlow 101. The local telephone directory was not a thick one, and if necessary I would go through every number. I looked into the passage, and listened; the only sounds were coming from downstairs, so I slipped out and re-locked the door with the little tool in my knife.

Once that was done I breathed more freely.

'Menlow 101,' I repeated to myself. 'Menlow 101.'

It was difficult to imagine mystery and crime in that little Wiltshire village.

A gentle wind was blowing along the High Street, and at the far end I saw Sheila and Elizabeth.

I walked towards them. A car was coming along the road behind me. I noticed that it slowed down, although I paid no attention. I was about fifty yards away from the others when it pulled up alongside me. I turned to look at the driver—and a shock went through me.

The dark moustache and dark eyebrows were unmistakably those which I had seen in London.

53

'You are very persistent,' he said, 'but take it from me this is no business of yours. Go back to London.'

The car moved off swiftly.

I saw Elizabeth and Sheila running towards the car. I shouted a warning, convinced that the driver would not hesitate to run over them. There could not have been more than ten feet between them and the car, which was putting on speed.

Sheila seemed to sway to one side, then fall to the ground. Elizabeth jumped clear as the car raced on, swung round a corner, and was lost to sight. Before I could reach Sheila's huddled body she had struggled to her feet.

My relief was enormous.

'What a crazy thing to do!' I exclaimed.

'I thought it might make him slow down,' said Sheila, shakily. 'What had he done to you?'

'Nothing much,' I said, 'except to make me look a fool.'

'Well, where can we go from here?' asked Elizabeth. 'There's no room at the George.'

'Nor at our pub,' I said. I gave them an outline of what had happened, adding irritably: 'Confound it, there must be somewhere we can stay!'

'What about a caravan?' suggested Elizabeth practically. 'I've some friends in Salisbury who used to have one.'

It was then just after half past ten, and a time-table outside our hotel showed that a bus for Salisbury was due at eleven-fifteen. Elizabeth declared that it would give her time to pack her things, and she strode off, quite determined to have her own way.

Sheila and I followed more leisurely.

None of us had again mentioned the car or the driver, and I was glad that Elizabeth was not going to insist on holding an inquest on everything that happened. I made up my mind to have lunch at the George and, while having a drink at the bar, to make inquiries about the man who looked like Farring.

'It's a great relief for Elizabeth to be doing something,' Sheila said.

'And a bigger one that we have a few hours to ourselves,' I said gleefully. 'Would that it were longer, for we'll have to start mixing with the natives as soon as the bar opens, to find out whether Farring has been here.' I seized her arm. 'Let's stroll out of the village and enjoy every minute, anyhow.'

All hopes of a quiet walk, however, were very soon dashed, for standing a few hundred yards from the last house in the village was a large bungalow with a sign outside, reading *Guest House*. Within seconds we were inquiring for accommodation. A flustered maid told us that they were already full up. Had we tried the George and the pub?

We said that we had.

'Well, you might find a room at Downs House,' she suggested doubtfully, 'but it's terribly expensive.'

It was not easy to break away, for the girl was of the rambling, loquacious kind, but we managed it at last. Nevertheless it was nearly twelve o'clock before we found ourselves striding in the direction she had given us.

Downs House turned out to be a large, creeper-clad Georgian building of very definite charm. If we had wanted a pleasant country holiday, it would have been an ideal place in which to stay.

A well-dressed, youngish woman swam forward as we entered.

'Good morning. Can I help you?'

55

'I hope you can,' I said, 'we are looking for accommodation.'

'For how many?'

'Three.'

'We have a double room and a single empty,' said the young woman, briskly, 'both rooms adjoining. For how long would you want to stay?'

'At least until after the weekend,' I said, hardly able to believe my ears.

'That would be all right,' she said, 'if you will wait just a moment I will get the keys and show you the rooms.'

Sheila and I regarded each other in amazed surprise. We were led briskly up a wide, carpeted staircase. The two rooms were at the end of a passage, immediately opposite a luxuriously fitted bathroom.

Indeed, the whole of Downs House was furnished luxuriously, the bedrooms being spacious and delightful, commanding views over hills and valley.

'Will these suit you?' asked the young woman, briskly.

'Admirably,' I said.

'Your terms?' Sheila said.

At any other country hotel I would have thought them stiff, but I would not have hesitated had they been twice as much.

To clinch the reservation we signed the register and filled out the necessary forms. There was no difficulty in getting luncheon, and we decided to fetch our luggage when Elizabeth returned from Salisbury, her bus being due about half past four. Neither of us seriously expected that she would get a caravan, and even if she did it might prove useful in an emergency.

No one was in the lounge.

We were sitting by the open French windows admiring

the grounds when the telephone rang. Some footsteps sounded on the stairs, and the voice of the receptionist, calm and assured, was wafted through to us.

'This is Menlow . . .' she said. I was not paying particular attention, and did not hear the number, except that the last figure was 'one'. Even then my curiosity would not have been roused but for the fact that she raised her voice.

'I am sorry, I can't hear you,' she said. 'This is Menlow 101.'

9

Elizabeth Triumphs

I did not recover from the shock of that discovery until after lunch, which was an excellent meal, well served, and accompanied by a half-bottle of claret. It was some time since I had been in a hotel where there was so little to remind one of the conditions ruling in England at that time.

'Darling,' said Sheila, gently, 'you aren't at your best.'

'But confound it, aren't you astonished?'

'Yes,' said Sheila, 'but I've got used to it.'

'If the fellow had the power to stop us from staying on at the little pub, why didn't he use his influence to keep us out of here?' I demanded.

'The frightened little man in the village and the owner of Downs House are very different propositions,' said Sheila. 'He might be able to frighten one but not the other. On the other hand . . .'

She paused, and as I stared at her I realised the obvious thing. It was clear that she had seen it from the first, but it had escaped me until then.

'You mean that he might have wanted us to come here?'

Sheila nodded.

It was clear enough then. As we were in Menlow, the man for whom we were looking would, naturally, prefer to have us where we could be kept under constant supervision. Once that train of thought had been set up, other possibilities followed, disquieting ones.

'The rooms weren't empty until yesterday,' I said, 'and yesterday was the day when Webb told us where Farring had been seen. I suppose it would be possible for Farring to have been allowed to walk about the village so that the police would learn where he was, and the rooms here emptied to make room for us.'

'That's a bit unlikely,' said Sheila.

'It is just possible,' I insisted. 'Darling, I'm going to get friendly with the hotel bore!'

'I'll come,' said Sheila, hastily.

We were not surprised to find the hotel lounge empty except for a pompous-looking man in plus-fours. He jumped up when he saw us and told Sheila that the settee in the corner by the fireplace was the most comfortable, and you got the best view of the garden from it. Unless she liked the afternoon sun, in which case the chair in the opposite corner would suit her best.

We thanked him, and took the settee.

'A delightful spot, this,' he declared, pathetically eager to impart information. 'My name is Blundell George Blundell—and yours, Mrs. . . .'

'Miss St. Clare,' said Sheila.

'Oh, I beg your pardon.' He turned to me. 'Perhaps you wife is coming later, Mr . . .'

'Deane,' said I. 'No, a friend is joining us.'

'Quite so, quite so. Now there are some very nice people here—although there are all sorts, you know, all sorts! You must be prepared for that.'

Thereupon he proceeded to give us the dossier of most of the hotel residents. I was less interested in the old-established residents than in those who had come recently, and by the time he had finished I had a fair picture of most of them.

The man he disliked most was a comparative newcomer who had been at Downs House for ten days. He was nothing but a dago, Blundell declared, though calling himself Raymond Seeley. He drew a picture of a tall, olive-skinned man who kept himself to himself. There was something unpleasant about the fellow, Blundell said. He was somewhere in the middle thirties, and ought to be in one of the services instead of travelling about the country buying up antiques.

I restrained a start of eagerness, listening with half an ear to the man's diatribe against antique furniture, but thinking far more of the sinister-looking fellow who was so happily labelled 'dago'. He could be an Italian, and there was every reason to believe that an Italian might be very interested in the Arturo Collection.

We left Blundell about half past three, not wanting to miss Elizabeth when she returned, well pleased with our progress. When we reached the village we found to our dismay that we had misread the time-table; the bus due in at half past four only ran on Saturdays and Tuesdays. The next bus back was at half past seven, and the twelve miles from Salisbury was beyond taxi radius.

It occurred to me then that it would be useful to have a car and a permit for petrol, so, on a letter-card obtained from the village post office, I wrote the request to Webb. The mail van came up as I finished and I was glad to be able to drop it into the bag.

'Elizabeth might get a lift out,' said Sheila, 'or else get on the better side of a taxi driver. One of us ought to stay here to make sure that we don't miss her.'

'We could leave a message at both hotels,' I said.

'I don't much like the idea,' said Sheila. 'We'll both have some tea at the George, anyhow, she might arrive by then.'

Elizabeth, however, was not back by five o'clock. Sheila and I stood outside the George, getting keyed up every time a car came in sight.

Then we heard the heavy sound of a lorry.

It came into sight, and behind it . . .

'She's got one!' I exclaimed.

Elizabeth, sitting beside the driver, grinned triumphantly. By then we could see the roof of a caravan. It looked enormous, and when it drew up outside the George we saw that it was a huge, cumbersome thing encrusted with the dirt and dust of years.

'This the place, mum?' asked the lorry driver.

Elizabeth called down composedly: 'Ned, have you fixed up a parking place?'

'Er—no, I . . .' I began.

Elizabeth swept a resigned glance towards Sheila. The next thing I knew was that the caravan had come to rest in a field adjoining the hotel, and Elizabeth was demanding pails of water, scrubbing brushes and floor-cloths.

'Inside it's a dream,' she declared. 'Four bunks, a sink and a table, and, what do you think, it's equipped with crockery and cutlery for three people!'

'Let's find someone in the village to clean it,' I suggested.

'They'd never do it in the time, and we have to sleep in it tonight.'

Then I broke the news to her about Downs House.

Though obviously disappointed, she took it reasonably enough. Nevertheless she was loath to capitulate entirely.

'We *might* need it tonight,' she said. 'We might be turned out of this place when they know who we are, or else there might be a fire. I think we ought to clean it now.'

We wrangled amiably about it as we collected our luggage, and, carrying a case apiece, walked towards Downs House. We had just turned into the drive, and Elizabeth was admitting that the place looked promising, when a car slowed down behind us.

The driver opened the window, and I recognised him instantly by Blundell's description.

The swarthy look, the dark eyes and furtive manner were unmistakable. Here was Blundell's 'dago'.

'Can I give you and your suitcases a lift, I'm going up to the hotel.'

We accepted gratefully for the luggage, and as the car went on its way, related to Elizabeth all Blundell had told us.

She made little comment, although the vivacity she had shown earlier faded.

'He is not a well-known dealer,' she said, abruptly.

'We only know that he's interested in antiques, not that he's a dealer,' I pointed out.

'If he were well known I would recognise him,' she said. 'What does he call himself? Raymond Seeley? I don't recognise the name. How do you propose to find out if he knows anything about my father?'

'We won't make the first approach,' I said.

'That's rather a negative method, isn't it?'

'What else can we do?' I demanded. 'Anyone who is connected with the mystery will know what we are trying to find out, and I expect to have a visitor before long. We've all the evidence we want that we have been either followed or awaited here.'

'You're right enough, I suppose. It's that man,' she added, and I was surprised to see her shiver. 'I didn't like the look of him.'

I said briskly: 'Come and see your room, and then have a hot bath. It will do you good and you'll get some of the caravan dust off you.'

Leaving Sheila to change her frock, I wandered off into the garden. Elizabeth might not like waiting, but I found it pleasant to have nothing in particular to do. Since working with Cris I have found the way to put things out of my mind until they are pressing, and although I don't always succeed, that evening I felt that we had made all the progress we could expect in one day, and it was certainly no use expecting the worst at every moment.

I went further than I intended, for the walks through the grounds were pleasant, and the grass was soft underfoot. I had not seen much of England in the last few months, and there is a quality about the English countryside which is soothing and satisfying, especially to the returned wanderer. I was not thinking about anything in particular when a shot startled me. Before moving swiftly behind a large beech tree I caught a glimpse of a man whom I took to be a gamekeeper.

He disappeared from sight.

To this day I do not know what made me go in the same direction, so that I caught a glimpse of him again as he fired the gun, for the second time. *It was pointing into the air!*

There seemed to be no sense in it, until it dawned on me that he had fired both shots as a warning.

I slipped along in his wake. Now I found my training in the French and Italian mountains a great asset, for I was able to take advantage of trees and bushes, with barely a sound.

Suddenly a cottage loomed out of the undergrowth. The man with the gun walked towards it, stood in the doorway for a moment as if to reassure himself that he had not been followed, then went in and closed the door. I stood watching.

The evening was quiet except for the trilling of birds and the persistent buzz of insects, but I was trained in dissociating such sounds from those caused by human agency, and it was not long before I heard footsteps. Presently, I saw two men approaching the cottage.

One I did not recognise, the other I took to be Leonard Farring.

10

I Make an Important Discovery

Farring and his companion were a hundred yards away from me. I could see their faces clearly. The art dealer looked pale and ill, and walked as if under compulsion.

The door closed again.

'Now we're getting somewhere!' I thought with satisfaction.

Had there been another man with Sheila and Elizabeth, I think I would have taken a chance and gone in after them. I did not like the idea of leaving the girls on their own, however, for there was a fair chance that I would not be allowed to leave the cottage alive.

So I waited.

After ten or fifteen minutes a man came out of the cottage and walked towards Downs House. Looking rather nervously round him, he passed within a few feet of me.

I thought that the gamekeeper was probably watching from the cottage window, so I made my way by a roundabout route to the drive, always keeping under cover. When I was within a few hundred yards of the house I saw the man approaching the shrubbery. He was a tall, well-built fellow of middle age, and now he was walking quickly and confidently, no longer casting covert glances over his shoulder.

As I entered the hotel by the front door the gong was sounding for dinner.

Sheila and Elizabeth appeared almost immediately, Sheila in a wine-red dress, Elizabeth in a long, green dinner-gown; I wondered how she had managed to cram so many clothes in so small a suitcase. I told them nothing, but when I went to the dining-room I chose a chair which enabled me to see every corner of the room.

It was not until after dinner, however, that I saw again the man I had followed back to the hotel.

He passed within an inch of us as Blundell was talking to me in the hall.

'That's Luke Orson, and a grand chap if ever there was one,' said Blundell. 'You wouldn't guess what he is in a thousand years!'

'What is he?' I asked, with a fair assumption of indifference. 'If he lives near here I'd say he was a gentleman farmer.'

'Then you'd be wrong,' said Blundell, with a chuckle, 'he's an artist. He has a cottage in the grounds and comes to the hotel for meals. I don't know much about painting myself, but he's marvellous at caricatures. You ought to see the one he did of me—it's up in my room.'

'I'd like to see it sometime,' I said hastily.

I wondered if Orson's cottage could be the one I had seen, but Blundell went on to say there were two, one of them rented by an old fellow who did a bit of fishing. He wasn't quite right in the head, but I need not be alarmed, however, for he was quite harmless, and in any case he always had a male nurse with him. He had only been at the cottage for a few weeks.

I went upstairs thoughtfully. Now that I knew that Farring was in the district, it seemed unnecessary to keep it from Elizabeth.

I told her that I had found out her father was living in a cottage in the grounds, and that the story was that he was recovering from a nervous collapse and needed constant attention, but that he seemed to be allowed a certain amount of freedom, and was well treated.

'So now we have two alternatives,' I finished. 'We can either tell the police what we know and doubtless arrange to get him away from them at once, or we can keep mum and investigate the matter ourselves.'

'I must talk to him,' Elizabeth said firmly.

'One of us must, and at the earliest opportunity,' I said, 'but not necessarily you.'

'I must talk to him before we tell the police,' said Elizabeth, and added challengingly: 'Why shouldn't I be the first? He is my father.'

'You forget that they can kidnap a daughter as easily as a father,' I said, 'and it will be better to keep one of the family free.' I looked at her thoughtfully. 'I don't know what is behind this, but it's a nasty business and we can't afford to take too many chances. The wise thing would be to advise Webb right away, but if you're set on finding out more from your father, then you'll have to work with me.'

I thought she would raise further objections, but she said, moving away, that she supposed I was right. I felt uneasy about her, half-afraid that she might take it into her head to roam the grounds and try to find where her father was.

'I don't think she'll do anything foolish,' Sheila said, reading my thoughts.

'I'm not sure that she trusts us,' I said thoughtfully. 'I think she's afraid that we'll keep the police informed too closely, and in that case she wouldn't hesitate to pull a fast one. I wish to heaven Cris was here!'

I broke off at a tap at the door, and Sheila called 'Come in.' The door opened, revealing Luke Orson.

He was a man who looked as if he were always completely sure of himself, but this time he was obviously taken aback. That he had not expected to see Sheila and me was clear enough.

He hesitated, trying to regain his composure.

'I'm so sorry, I think I have come to the wrong room. I am looking for Miss Farring.'

'This is her room,' I said. 'She is sharing it with Miss St. Clare. Can we take a message?'

'So kind of you, but no, I needn't trouble you for that.'

I watched him until he was about to turn round, and then said: 'Miss Farring knows that her father is here.'

Orson stopped. The air of embarrassment faded, and I needed no more telling that he was a man to be reckoned with.

'Who told her?' he asked.

'I did,' I said.

Orson closed the door, and came further into the room. In spite of the circumstances, I had a favourable impression of him. He was exceedingly good-looking in a rugged way, and it would not be difficult to imagine women liking him very much indeed.

'I don't know who you are,' he said evenly, 'but presumably you are a friend of Miss Farring, perhaps of Mr. Farring.' He paused, waiting for confirmation, but I said nothing. 'If you are, I give you a piece of advice and my strong recommendation that you take it. Go away from here and don't make Farring's position more dangerous than it is.'

'Dangerous?' I said, as if surprised.

'It is extremely dangerous,' said Orson. 'I have been a close friend of Leonard Farring's for many years, and I am trying to save him from disaster. If you have any influence with his daughter, persuade her to leave here.'

'I shall do nothing of the kind,' I said.

'Then you are no friend of the Farrings,' he declared.

He turned on his heel, and the door closed firmly behind him. I took a step towards it, but stopped when I heard Elizabeth's voice outside the door. Orson was asking if he could speak to her, and she was assenting.

A door opened and closed.

I stood indecisively. It was easy to imagine a man like Orson talking plausibly enough to convince her— for she was already half-convinced—that interference would only worsen her father's position. When I heard them going downstairs, I decided to follow them.

I was just in time to see them disappearing in the direction of the cottage which I had seen across clear patches of grassland beyond the shrubbery. Soon I was near enough to see the path along which the gamekeeper had walked. Hardly had I reached a convenient clump of bushes when a shot rang out.

I stood still.

Suddenly I caught a glimpse of the gamekeeper. He waited until the others had passed him, then followed.

I thought it unlikely that he suspected my presence and, taking as much advantage of tree cover as I could, I approached the cottage.

The gamekeeper stopped not far away, and took up a position behind a patch of bramble. Stealthily, and with utmost care—for the man only had to catch a glimpse of me and there would be no chance at all of achieving my object—I reached the garden at the back of the cottage. No one appeared to be near the windows, and I took a chance and walked boldly forward until I was close to the wall. I waited, but there was no indication that I had been seen.

I approached the nearest window cautiously, and peered in. The room beyond was a kitchen, and it was empty. The next was a sitting-room.

When I reached the front windows, the gamekeeper was still peering in the other direction; he would not be likely to look at the cottage itself. There was no cover, and I had to stand my chance of being seen.

I looked through the window of a little dining-room, and no one was there; the other room at the front was furnished as a study, and the walls were lined with books. No one was in either room.

'So that's that,' I murmured.

I had no liking for burglary, but I meant to find out what was being said in that cottage, so I tried the latch of the front door. It opened and I stepped inside.

The stairs, narrow and crooked, led from the middle of the wall on the right-hand side. I crept up, bending my head to avoid the low ceiling.

From the moment I set foot in the hall I heard voices, and these grew louder as I went upstairs.

'No, my dear, these people are quite right. There is nothing we can do but be patient. Tell these good friends of yours not to worry on my account.'

'But they are working for the police!' exclaimed Elizabeth, 'they'll have to report finding you here!'

Farring said: 'Somehow or other, Elizabeth, you must stop them.'

I heard Elizabeth exclaim, and I could sympathise with her. My own bewilderment at finding her father a willing, or at least an unprotesting, captive was tempered by the insecurity of my own position. I retreated a little further down the stairs, to lessen the likelihood of being seen. The lower rooms appeared to be quite deserted, but someone might come in the back way.

I thought I heard footsteps, and waited tensely, but nothing further materialised. The distraction made me miss something that was said, but next I heard Orson speaking, his deep, rather attractive voice perfectly clear.

'I give you my assurance, Miss Farring, that no further danger is likely if you persuade Deane to go away from here and prevent him from reporting to the police. If the police do come . . .' He broke off, then continued: 'I can promise nothing.'

'But *who* is doing this? Who . . . ?'

'It's better for you not to know,' said Orson gravely. 'It would only make more trouble for yourself. It's a thousand pities that you ever came down here. How did Deane find out about Menlow?'

I waited, breathlessly.

'I don't know,' said Elizabeth.

I warmed towards her for not letting me down, wondering how this situation would work out; it was becoming more involved, and behind it there appeared to be fear on the part of Farring and Orson of some unnamed person. I was by no means sure that Orson was the victim of circumstances which he made himself out to be; he might be playing a double game, and be setting out to disarm Elizabeth; certainly he wanted her to keep silent.

Orson spoke next.

'Does Deane know that it might be dangerous for him?'

'Of course he does! He saw what happened to Reccivi.'

'I am afraid that Reccivi discovered more than we thought,' said Orson. 'Well, we mustn't stay here. I hope you're convinced that you must somehow prevail upon Deane to be helpful.'

'I don't see how I can,' said Elizabeth.

'You must find a way,' said Orson, and added: 'I'll wait for you downstairs.'

I had not heard him approaching the door, and backed down the stairs hastily. I managed to slip through the doorway of the book-lined room, as Orson entered the hall.

He walked towards me, and for a moment I was afraid that he was coming in. Instead, he stood just outside the door. I supposed that he intended to allow the others to have five minutes together, on their own— and then all thought of what was happening in the cottage faded, for from the garden there came the now familiar roar of a shotgun.

Orson stepped swiftly to the front door, and opened it. I approached the window cautiously.

The gamekeeper was now in sight, walking towards the cottage with his gun under his arm.

'Who is it?' asked Orson. 'Deane?'

'No, I haven't seen him.'

'Then who is it?'

'I don't know,' said the gamekeeper. 'I—ah! There he is!'

A man passed between two clumps of bushes, disappearing in a flash. The dark hair suggested Seeley, but if it were the dealer in antiques he had changed his clothes, for this man was dressed in brown.

'I'll deal with him,' said the gamekeeper. Thin-faced and bitter-looking he strode past the window.

Suddenly the quiet of the night was broken by the sharp report of a shot, and I knew that it was not from the shotgun. Orson ran from the house, while I peered rashly from the window.

The gamekeeper was stretched out on the ground, a hundred yards away, and Orson was running towards him.

11

I Take an Exceptional Opportunity

What happened to the gamekeeper was no affair of mine. I knew that I was not likely to have such an opportunity of interviewing Farring again, and if I caught the man by surprise he might make some disclosure and give me the key to what was behind this mystery.

Before I reached the stairs, however, I heard Elizabeth descending them. Her head was held high and her cheeks were flushed; I needed no telling that the private talk with her father had not been helpful. She went out, and I doubled back on my tracks.

I waited for a moment outside Farring's door, then without tapping I went inside.

Farring was sitting in an easy chair, staring towards

the window. It was a bedroom; I noticed that, but for the rest I had eyes only for Farring.

I have never seen such a look of hopelessness on a man's face. The fine forehead, from which the grey hair swept back, was lined with furrows, his lips drooped and his body sagged.

As I stepped towards him, he turned and faced me.

I doubt whether he realised who I was; I don't think he would have recognised anyone, for he was so obsessed with his own thoughts; perhaps his own fears.

'Don't worry me now,' he said.

'I'm sorry ...' I began.

'I will see you later!' said Farring, with more power in his voice; and then he stopped, for he realised that I was a stranger.

'My name is Deane,' I said.

He did not speak.

'Mr. Farring,' I said, 'I heard something of what you told your daughter, but ...'

I could not go on, for he started to get up, moving as if it pained him. There was a determined glint in his eyes.

'Mr. Deane, you are not wanted here. I do not want your help, nor that of the police. I demand the right of every man to do what he wishes, provided it is within the law.'

'That you are doing so is hard to believe,' I said.

He took a step towards me, as if to implore me to pay heed to what he was going to say.

'I beg of you to take no further interest in this unhappy business. If you do, your own safety and that of my daughter might be endangered. I beg you to go away, to forget that you have ever seen me!'

I said: 'Listen, Farring, you need help and I can help you. There is no need for me to make any report to the police, I can use my own judgement as to whether that's necessary. Tell me what is the matter, and I'll help in every way I can, for your daughter's sake if not your own.'

'*No* one can help,' said Farring.

'That's nonsense! At least one man has been killed . . .'

'That is a lie!' he snapped more vigorously. 'I have not made these sacrifices in order to allow men to die!'

'At least one has been killed and Reccivi may die,' I said, and added grimly: 'Nothing you can do will bring Forbes back to life, nor alter the fact that he was murdered because he had for sale a painting which was held in trust by you.'

He stared at me like a man in a daze.

He repeated: '*Forbes* back to life?'

'Yes,' I said, crisply, 'does it surprise you that he is dead.'

He said: 'If Forbes is dead, *anything* may happen.'

The words seemed over-dramatised then; it was not until afterwards that I gave them serious thought, and realised how much they might mean. At the moment I believed that he was trying to sidetrack me, and I spoke sharply.

'Anything, yes—including the death of your daughter.'

'She will not be hurt unless she interferes,' he said. 'I have made that clear to her, and now I will make it clear to you. I have no doubt that your intentions are excellent, but if you persist in your inquiries you will be appalled at the consequences. I beg you . . .'

Then a door banged downstairs.

I was so engrossed in the conversation with Farring that I was forgetful of the danger. I turned towards the door as someone came running upstairs. Another door opened, and I heard Orson's voice:

'Where *is* the damned stuff?'

Farring was staring at me.

I did not know what to make of his expression. I stepped towards the door as Orson hurried downstairs, carrying a red cross box in his hand.

I followed him.

He turned into the study, leaving the door open. The gamekeeper lay stretched out on a settee. Elizabeth was bending over him, and the man who had acted as Farring's warder when I had first seen the antique dealer was standing near.

As I watched, a mad notion passed through my mind; while they were so preoccupied I could go upstairs and force Farring to leave the cottage. Once he was at Downs House he could be guarded, and I could telephone Webb and tell him that my quest was finished. I think I might have tried to put that into operation but for the memory of Farring's expression. Instead, I slipped out through the front door to the back of the house, from where I had a circuituous route back towards the hotel. It was not long before I knew that I was being followed.

After a few minutes I paused to light a cigarette. Out of the tail of my eye I saw the brown-clad, dark-haired man who had come in sight just before the gamekeeper had been shot.

It was Seeley.

I was tempted to force an issue with him, but voices nearby stopped me. Two couples whom I had seen in the dining-room passed within a few yards, and as I stood aside they wished me good evening. It was now dusk, and in a little while it would be too dark to play hide-and-seek in the grounds. Seeley had moved further into the trees, and there was nothing for it but to go back to the hotel. I had discovered enough for one evening, and I wanted to marshal my thoughts.

I wished more than ever that Cris were at hand.

As I entered the front door of the hotel, the efficient reception clerk came from the office.

'Good evening, sir. Miss St. Clare has gone out, and left a message for you. She is meeting Mr. Anson at the George and would like you to go on there.'

'Mr. Anson?' I said, puzzled.

'That was the name,' said the girl, briskly. 'Would you like morning tea?'

'Er—yes. Yes please,' I added, trying to gather my wits. 'Thank you. I . . .'

'What time, sir, please?'

'Eight o'clock,' I said.

I hurried up to my own room.

Who the deuce was 'Mr. Anson'? Racking my brains in search of someone of that name, I was plagued with doubts and anxieties. It would be the easiest thing in the world to lure Sheila away with a false message, and for all I knew she might have walked into danger. Almost frantic with anxiety, I went downstairs again and telephoned the George.

Sheila was not there, and although I gave her description to the clerk and a request that he would look in the bar, he returned with the same message. I hurried to the office and asked where I could get a taxi. The receptionist said that I was not likely to get one so late in the evening, without booking earlier in the day.

I set out to walk.

Although I had only been in the hotel for a few minutes, it was much darker when I went out again and hurried along the drive. I imagined myself being watched by several pairs of eyes, and once when someone jumped down from the grass verge on to the gravel of the drive I nearly jumped out of my skin.

'Hallo, hallo, there!' boomed Blundell. 'Taking a constitutional?'

I hurried past, calling 'Good night.'

Even that encounter and its outcome left me a prey to nerves, and as I reached the end of the drive a cyclist, without lights, rode past. I jumped again, and then told myself that it was time I stopped being a fool. I walked swiftly along the main road.

Figures suddenly loomed out of the gloom in front of me, and I thought I recognised Sheila's voice. I stood quite still, and a moment later I was sure.

Here, walking towards me and talking excitedly, were Sheila and Anton. If Cris could not be here, there was no man I would rather have than Anton Duval.

'Ned, *mon ami*!' Before I knew what he intended Anton had flung his arms about me and kissed me resoundingly on either cheek. 'Let me see you—ah! A worried look, even when it is so dark I can see enough for that. Trouble for *M'sieu* Deane—Sheila,' he added reproachfully, 'you did not tell me.'

No one says 'Sheila' quite like Anton. He makes the first syllable short and the second one emphatic, as if he loved the name and wanted to get the most out of it. Once I thought him a serious rival; in fact I could not imagine what Sheila could see in me, when Anton was dancing attendance on her, but she had told me, laughing, that if anyone but a Frenchwoman married Anton, it would be a tragedy. He was engaged now to a girl whom he had brought safely from France during one of our shows there, but he had not lost his roving eye.

'You ass!' I said. 'Seriously, how did you get here?'

'Even in your wonderful country there are ears where one expects none,' said Anton. 'If this affair is the great mystery which Sheila makes out, then we should converse about it only when we can be sure that we are not overheard. Already you have been indiscreet!'

Anton was pulling my leg, but as we walked back towards Downs House I was uncomfortably aware of the fact that he was right. I should not have seemed so surprised, nor asked him how he had found out where we were staying. If anyone had overheard me, it would give the lie to any later statement I might want to make.

This realisation affected my better spirits for a few minutes, although Sheila slipped her arm through mine and Anton walked on her other side, talking gaily.

Presently he whispered to me: 'There is someone behind us!'

As we reached the steps of the hotel, he turned and disappeared. Quite literally, he was there one second and gone the next. I did not even know which way he went, and I stood indecisively at the top of the steps, peering into the darkness, feeling the pressure of Sheila's arm by my side.

'We'd better go in,' I said. 'You go upstairs, they'll think you've gone with Anton.'

I felt her lips brush against my cheek, and the next moment she was opening the door. I smiled to myself as we went in and she hurried up the stairs, waving to me from the first landing. I don't think she will ever know how much moments like that meant to me.

The door opened a few minutes afterwards, and Seeley came in.

He had changed from brown tweeds to a formal suit, and walked past me quickly, with an absent smile.

Anton came in almost immediately afterwards.

'So, there you are, Ned! Have you arranged my room for me?'

'No, I . . .'

The receptionist appeared, as if summoned by some mechanical means, at the office door.

'I'm sorry, sir, we have no vacancy.'

It had not occurred to me before that there might not be room for Anton; the wand had been waved so generously that I had taken it for granted that he would be able to stay here. Immediately I foresaw great difficulties, but Anton smiled upon the girl, and under such Gallic pressure she promised to see the manager.

He turned out to be a portly, middle-aged man with a friendly manner and a cultured voice very carefully acquired. I was putting him in a delicate position, he said, for there was a single room vacant but it was reserved for a regular guest, who might come that night. He suggested that I should try the other hotels.

'They were all full up this morning,' I said.

'Were they, indeed. It is most unfortunate.'

We stood looking at each other.

'Can you put an extra bed in my room?' I suggested.

'That *would* be a solution to the problem,' admitted the manager, as if it were a completely new idea. 'May we leave it that we will do just that, unless we hear something definite from our other guest?'

Going upstairs, Anton whispered: 'Nothing is impossible, Ned!'

'So it seems,' I said, 'but we don't want to hear what a wonderful man you are at the moment, there are other things to talk about.'

'That is jealousy,' declared Anton.

When I tapped on the door of Sheila's room and we went in, he became more serious.

I plunged into my story, and Anton's grave face and Sheila's tense look proved that it gripped them. Until then I had not been able to get everything clear in my mind, but as I talked every incident became vivid. There

78

was Elizabeth's set face as she had come from her father's room, the antique dealer sitting in his corner with that desolate expression, the shooting, the shot gamekeeper. By finishing with the story of Seeley in his brown suit, I reached the point at which Anton had gone away to look for him.

'He waited until he thought we were all in, and then walked up the stairs,' said Anton. 'I did not see him, of course, but one thing I will guarantee—I shall recognise him again by the pomade he uses.'

He meditated for a moment, and then said: 'So! they have a willing prisoner!'

I was used to the bewildering suddenness with which Anton changed the subject, and nodded thoughtfully.

'It makes the situation more involved,' said Sheila.

'It is a matter of great interest,' admitted Anton. 'I am glad that I was asked to take a share in it, Ned!'

'That's what's been on my mind,' I said. 'How did you get down here?'

It was simple enough. Returning to England several days earlier than expected, he had see Clyde who had passed on the details of the story. Anton had caught the first train from Waterloo.

'Also, I telephoned the small inn where you stayed last night, and booked a room!'

'Well, I'm damned!' I said.

'It was better for me to be here with you.'

'But if you were staying there we could have compared notes from time to time,' I protested, 'and we could always have brought in the element of surprise. You made a mistake there, Anton!'

He grinned.

'The element of surprise, now—wait for it! It is Cris who will be staying at that inn, and the name under which the room is booked is Carey, so they will not know him!'

I was so delighted to hear that Cris was on his way, and so eager to find out how he had managed to get out of France, that I forgot one obvious thing: anyone who saw Cris and knew Sheila would realise that they were brother and sister.

12

In Which Elizabeth is Difficult

The difficulties which the likeness between Sheila and Cris might cause occurred to me while I was sitting in the dining-room and Anton was having dinner. The cooking at Downs House was excellent and Anton did the meal full justice. Sheila was upstairs, and was coming to tell me immediately Elizabeth returned.

Anton glanced at me suddenly.

'Ned, you have had an uncomfortable thought!'

'I have,' I said. 'Anyone seeing Cris will know he's Sheila's brother, so much for the secrecy!'

'*Nom d'un nom*, that is right!' Anton looked dismayed.

'Well, it's too late to do anything about it now,' I said. 'With the three of us together we shall stand a much better chance of getting results. So many mysterious things are happening. For instance, I'm not at all sure the manager is clear of suspicion. I got a distinct impression that there *is* a room available but that he wanted to consult someone else before letting you have it.'

'No, no!' said Anton, who was never depressed for long. 'He raised no objection to the extra bed in your room.'

'That's true, but we're all nicely tucked away in one corner,' I said.

'The truth, Ned, is that you are worried by the way things are going,' said Anton. 'I think perhaps you did not express all your fears when Sheila was with us. Perhaps you were wise, but I do not think there is much point in hiding things from her. What she does not know she will guess, *mon ami*.'

'I suppose so,' I admitted, 'but I hate to have her worried. The thing which worries me most,' I added, 'is the fact that the gamekeeper was shot.'

Anton nodded.

Both of us realised that it meant that there was a third party interested in this mystery of Farring. First there was Farring himself, and with him I put Luke Orson, the gamekeeper, the warder fellow and someone unknown. Earlier in the evening I had added Seeley to that list, and even suspected that Seeley was the unnamed man, but I doubted that now, for it seemed probable that Seeley had shot the gamekeeper to prevent himself from being discovered. Even if Seeley was innocent of the shooting, someone had fired the shot and that someone I put into the second category; there would be other members of it, probably, and it seemed likely that Farring might be held a prisoner to save him from attacks such as that on the gamekeeper.

Anton admitted that possibility, which in some measure might explain the way Farring behaved.

The third category was a large one; it included Reccivi, the murdered Forbes, Superintendent Webb, Sheila, Anton, Cris, Elizabeth and myself. By stretching the imagination a little I could put Clyde into the category, too; all the people in it were anxious to find out not only what had happened to Farring, but *why* it had happened. I was wondering how it was that Clyde had sent Anton and Cris down so quickly when another thought flashed through my mind. Webb knew that Farring was down here, and he might also know something of the circumstances; he was far less interested in what was happening to Farring than in the reason for it. Probably he had asked me to come down because he did not want to take any official action at this juncture, and his own men could not have behaved with Farring as I had done.

Anton also agreed that this was probable.

'Did you get any idea why Clyde was so willing for us to help the police?' I asked him.

'I would not say that I had an idea,' he said, 'but I would not be surprised to find that Clyde considers it important, Ned. It is a curious situation, you understand—this great collection of Italian masterpieces is extremely valuable. I think Clyde is afraid that Italian interests, inimicable towards the Allies, might be behind it.'

'I'd wondered about that,' I admitted.

Anton poured himself a second cup of coffee. He was drinking it when the door opened and, looking round, I saw Sheila.

I pushed my chair back.

'Elizabeth's upstairs,' Sheila said, at once, 'she went straight to your room, Ned.'

'Such boldness!' exclaimed Anton.

'This isn't funny,' I said. 'She doesn't know that you're about, Anton, you'd better stay in the background for a little while.'

'But wait! Would it not be better, perhaps, if you allowed me to question her? Finesse is of some importance, and you were never good at handling women!'

I could not rebut that, because it was perfectly true. I felt ruffled as I went upstairs, the others following me; it seemed to me that everyone was intent on pointing out my shortcomings. My chagrin lasted only for a short time, however.

Elizabeth was sitting facing me as I opened the door, and I was taken aback by her expression. It was a reflection of the despair which I had seen in her father only a few hours earlier.

'I've been waiting for you,' she said listlessly.

'Where have you been?' I asked.

'To see my father.'

'You shouldn't have gone, Elizabeth,' I said. 'I knew it would be folly.'

'I had to see him. Luke Orson, a man who is staying here, took me. Ned, I'm desperately sorry, but we can't go on.'

'Now that . . .' I began.

'We can't go on!' she repeated fiercely. 'There's nothing you or I or the police can do that will help my father now. Later, perhaps, someone might be able to help, but just now we can do nothing. Ned'—she stood up abruptly—'I hate asking you to do this, but I want you to telephone the police, and tell them you have found out nothing. Stay here for a few days, and then go back and say it's a waste of time and you are not going on with it.'

'Now, come!' I said. 'The fact that your father is detained near here, against his will . . .'

'It isn't against his will!' She gripped my hand, and I was surprised at her strength. 'He's quite willing to stay here. I'm so frightened that if we go on with it something dreadful will happen to him.'

'You're making it very difficult,' I said.

'I'm not! It would be easy enough, if you'd agree to deceiving the police. I know that you and Sheila were going on holiday, you'd much rather spend the next ten days with her than be here with all these things happening. Ned, don't be obstinate, and don't think that I don't appreciate all you've done and tried to do. It's more than good of you and I'm really grateful.'

I released my hand and stepped back from her. I could see that she was intensely serious and that something she had been told had really frightened her. Nothing her father had said to me would have caused this attitude on her part.

I said: 'Elizabeth, it can't be done. I think that severe pressure is being brought on your father to make him complaisant. Crime is an ugly thing, and this one has to be stopped.'

'What do you mean?' she flashed. 'It's happened already!'

'Oh, no,' I said. 'Something is being planned, probably something pretty fiendish. It's gone too far for me to back out now. The best I can do is to keep developments from the police until we can give them the whole story. At the moment your father seems to be implicated, but later there might be a satisfying reason for his attitude. I'm here for the duration, my dear, and I have friends who are coming to help.'

'They must go back!' she cried.

I said shortly: 'You're talking like a hysterical schoolgirl!'

She flushed, and turned away. I wondered if I had gone too far, but her voice was less taut when she spoke again.

'If you'd seen my father . . .'

'I have seen him,' I said, abruptly, 'and I saw enough

to be quite sure that we can't allow things to go on like this. Elizabeth, what did he tell you?'

I don't think she heard the question.

'When did you see him?'

'I was at the cottage, and went in after you had come out,' I said shortly. 'None of them knew that I had been there. The only man who might have seen me was the gamekeeper—is he still alive, by the way?'

She had gone chalk white, and when she answered her voice was pitched on a high key.

'Yes, of course he's alive! It was only a scratch!'

'That's good,' I said, 'because if there had been more murder, it would have been difficult to keep away from the police just now.'

'You must not tell them what happened, you mustn't tell them that you've seen my father!'

'I think the best thing we can do is to sleep on it,' I said, 'you'll probably see things differently in the morning. Are you coming in to see Sheila now? She's with a friend we've mentioned, I think—Anton Duval.'

'I—I'll come in later,' she said.

I was glad to get away, and I stood outside the other door for a few seconds, taking command of myself.

Anton greeted me with his usual persiflage.

'Well, Ned?' he demanded. 'Have you handled the Amazon in your usual he-man fashion?'

'Listen to me,' I said. 'The gamekeeper died. Elizabeth told me that it was only a scratch, but she seemed terrified when I mentioned him and I have no doubt that he's dead and that they're going to hush the murder up. As they didn't commit it themselves, that's proof enough that all of them, including Orson, are frightened out of their lives. When someone can commit cold-blooded murder like that and get other people to cover it up because they're scared, it's time we got moving.

There's another thing. I think she'll tell Orson that I know, and it's just possible that we ourselves will be in acute danger. Sheila, go in next door, will you, and at all costs stop Elizabeth form talking to anyone else until we're back.'

'What are you going to do?'

'I want to find out what they've done with the body,' I said grimly.

Sheila raised no objection, and in a few minutes Anton and I went downstairs, feeling fairly sure that she would be able to handle Elizabeth. I was still very much on edge, certain that my visit to the cottage, now that Elizabeth knew of it, would quicken the tempo of the affair.

It was pitch dark outside.

'Just what are you going to do?' asked Anton, in a whisper.

'Visit the cottage,' I said.

I don't really know why I was so sure that we had to go to the cottage, unless it was that I wanted to make sure that the gamekeeper was dead.

I led the way through a tangle of bushes and shrubs. There was a faint glow of light coming from the cottage, and at sight of it I stood still, with a hand on Anton's arm.

There was no wind, but now and again I heard a rustle of movement. From the moment we had left the hotel I thought that we were followed. Anton realised what I suspected, and made no sound.

The door of the cottage opened and the shadowy forms of three men appeared.

They did not come towards us, and I began to move in their direction. I was quite sure that whoever was watching us also moved. I thought that in all probability it was Seeley, and that it was he who had shot the gamekeeper.

The party which had left the cottage walked for two or three hundred yards, and then stopped. A torch light shone fleetingly on a mound of earth. A grave. Before the light went out, a body was lowered into it.

Neither Anton nor I moved, and as we stood there the sound of shovelled earth came clearly to us. I suppose the whole business took about twenty minutes, before the men turned back towards the cottage.

I thought for a moment, and then turned to Anton:

'Perhaps you'd better get back to the hotel and make sure that Sheila's all right, I'm not too happy about her being there. I wish I knew who was in this business and who wasn't,' I added, irritably.

'Would it be better if I saw Orson?' Anton suggested. 'I will create more effect, perhaps, because he does not know me.'

'I think I'd better see him,' I said.

Anton had not seriously expected to be able to force me from my purpose, and he raised no further protest. We went back towards the hotel together. I had little doubt that Orson was one of the men who had attended that furtive burial. He would probably stay at the smaller cottage for a little while, and if I were waiting for him when he reached his own, the effect would be much greater.

I left Anton near the hotel.

When he had gone, I moved a few yards along the drive and then stopped, for I saw a sliver of light from the top of a window. As far as I could judge, that was where Orson's cottage should be.

I went forward cautiously. I did not think Orson would be back yet, and for a moment I thought that perhaps no one had any right in the house. That was absurd, I told myself, for he would have servants.

Then I wondered if I were right; he came to the hotel for all meals, and I thought Blundell had told me he had only a daily woman. True, he might have friends staying there, and it would be folly to jump to conclusions.

I drew within a few feet of the light, and I saw that it came from a ground-floor window, partially open. I crept forward, and listened; I heard the sounds of movement, as if a drawer was being pulled open.

Slowly, inch by inch, I put my hand inside the room and touched the curtain. I was desperately anxious to make no noise and it took a long time to get the curtain back far enough to see into the room.

Then I saw a shadow on the wall.

It was of a man who appeared to be bending down. One thing was certain, all his attention was on what he was doing, and unless I made a noise he would not turn to look towards the window.

I pulled the curtain a little further aside, until I was able to see him.

It was Seeley, and he was bending over a bureau-desk, with an intent expression on his swarthy face. I noticed that several papers were on one side, as if he had selected them to take away.

Then, without warning, something crashed upon my head. I remember the sickening pain of the blow, before everything faded.

Luke Orson Acts the Good Samaritan

When I came round I was in a room.

My head was aching abominably, and the light hurt my eyes. I closed them, setting my teeth against the pain.

Yet I had seen enough to know that there was something vaguely familiar about the room. Could it be the one in which Seeley had been searching for papers? There was no sign of him now. I opened my eyes again and saw the bureau, the drawer of which was open. There was other evidence that the room had been searched; cushions were on the floor, a small table was on its side, and several pictures were leaning against the wall, where they had been taken from their hooks.

I do not know how long I stayed there, trying to summon up enough strength to move.

The I heard footsteps approaching.

They were firm and deliberate. They stopped and were followed by a scratching sound, probably that of a key being inserted in the lock of the front door. I tried to sit up, half-fainting with the effort.

Then the door was flung open and Orson came in.

He did not see me immediately. I saw his expression alter when he saw the rifled bureau, and he stepped across swiftly, bent down, and put his hand inside the top drawer. I must have made some movement, for he swung round.

He stared at me in amazement.

Afterwards I admired the way in which he handled the situation, and the speed with which he recovered from his surprise.

He looked at me critically.

'You're not badly hurt,' he said, and I was quite sure of the note of relief in his voice. 'You'll be all right.'

'I'm thirsty,' I muttered.

'I'll get some water,' said Orson. 'Don't move, or you'll suffer for it!'

He came back quickly with a glass of water, which he held to my lips with evident concern.

He went out again and came back with a small bottle.

'Aspirins,' he said briefly. He showed me the label, and I took three of the tablets, helping them down with another sip of water.

'Now close your eyes for ten minutes,' he said.

'That's a—hell of a—bright light,' I said.

'I'll fix it,' said Orson.

No one could have been more considerate nor more thoughtful. He went to the door and switched off the light, so that only a glow came from the hall. Then he switched on a table lamp, after first draping a handkerchief over it.

I closed my eyes again; and for ten minutes I do not think I would have cared what anyone did. After a while I began to think more clearly, remembering that Orson's first thought had been for the bureau. Then I thought that he was behaving remarkably well; I had always thought him a likable man, in spite of what had happened. I began to wonder what he would say if I said, suddenly, that I had seen him burying the game-keeper's body. That was getting near to hysteria, and I opened my eyes slowly.

Orson was sitting on an upright chair, facing me. When he saw my eyes open he smiled.

'Feeling better?'

'A little,' I admitted, cautiously.

'A cup of tea won't do you any harm,' he said. 'I've got a kettle on.'

He went out, returning in a few minutes with a pot of tea and two cups on a small tray. He poured out, then helped me to sit up.

'I shouldn't move too much,' he said comfortably. 'That crack over the head would have put most men out for a week! Who did it?'

'I don't know.'

Orson said: 'You must admit, Deane, I did my best to warn you.'

'I know,' I said, and grimaced. 'I thought I was better than I am. It won't happen again.'

'It certainly won't,' he said. 'Next time they'll make a job of it.'

'You take too grim a view,' I said.

Provided I talked without opening my lips too much I was in reasonable comfort. I was trying to make up my mind how much to tell Orson, and decided that it would be wiser to say as little as possible. So when he asked me how I had come to be in the room, I told him that I wanted to talk to him and, on the way, had noticed the light and the open window and looked in. I did not have to pretend anything about the blow over the head. He looked at me grimly.

'Who was in here? Seeley?'

I shrugged non-committally.

'What do you know about Seeley?' he asked.

'Only what Blundell told me.'

'Oh, that garrulous ass! Nothing Blundell says is anything but gossip.'

'He didn't like Seeley, and I can't say that I do,' I said.

'Nor would anyone with any sense,' said Orson. 'Did the police warn you about him?'

91

'They did not,' I said. It looked as if Orson also thought that he might get a lot out of the interview, and I could hardly blame him for taking advantage of my weakness.

He said abruptly: 'Deane, are you a regular police officer?'

I think my stare of astonishment was a sufficient answer. He looked as if he had come to a big decision as he pulled his chair closer to me, and said earnestly:

'If you're not, I think you might be able to help us. I'm tired to death of this hole-and-corner business. How much do you know about it?'

'Little enough,' I said, and told him as much as I thought was good for him. Although my head was still aching, the painful throbbing had lessened and I was able to give him full attention. I finished up with: 'As far as I can see the Farrings are making a pretty thorny nest for themselves, especially Elizabeth.'

I thought there was a harsher note in his voice, as if I had said something which was distasteful.

'I know. I thought it best to try to bring her round to her father's way of thinking, but ever since this business started I have been doing what I thought was the best, and it's turned out badly. Look here, Deane, I've sworn by everything I hold sacred that I will not tell the police what I know. If you are a police officer . . .'

'Hold tight!' I protested. 'I've already told you that I'm not. In fact I was puzzled as to why the police asked me to help them. They must have a dozen capable officers who could do a better job than I can. There appeared only one reasonable explanation, and that is that they know there is something which Farring will not tell them, but they think I might be able to make him more amenable. I think they realise that there is a serious crime being planned, and they don't mind working through me—they think I might keep some things back about Farring, but that I won't let anything go seriously amiss. Have I made myself clear?' I added, feeling that I could not have been much more involved.

Orson drew in his breath sharply.

'All right, Deane, I'll take a chance with you.'

'That's the sensible thing to do,' I said, trying to hide my elation. 'I have friends who will lend a hand, and as far as I can see you need all the help you can get.'

'I do, by George!' said Orson. 'I . . .'

And then, of all times, I heard footsteps outside, and I saw Orson turn towards the window. He stood up without a word as the door bell rang.

I sat fuming. Whoever it was might make him think again, even if they did nothing to try to make him change his mind. He was a long time opening the door, and then I heard him exclaim:

'Miss Farring!'

'Let me come in,' said Elizabeth sharply. The door closed and I could hear her heavy breathing. 'I've only just managed to get away. Deane's fiancée tried to keep me, but I slipped out. Deane was at the cottage when the gamekeeper was shot, and he saw my father!'

Orson did not answer.

I drew in my breath, and prepared for an unpleasant ten minutes. As Orson had been prepared to be frank, he might reasonably have expected me to have told him that much, and in any case it might be enough to make him change his mind.

'Well, can't you say something?' demanded Elizabeth.

'Deane is here, rather knocked about,' said Orson.

'*Here!*'

'Yes. Come in, Miss Farring.'

She entered the room, the pallor of her cheeks making her eyes seem unnaturally bright. As he followed her, I could not help thinking what a fine couple they made, being much of a height and having something of the same quality.

Her expression altered when she saw me.

'Ned, you're hurt!'

'Orson tells me that it looks worse than it is,' I said.

He said slowly: 'So you know about the gamekeeper, Deane?'

What sense was there in keeping anything back?

'Yes,' I said wearily, 'and I know where he is buried.'

If he were one of the rogues, acting like this to deceive and disarm Elizabeth, I had burned my boats with a vengeance. I did not think he was, but I knew enough about the violence of this business to realise, too late, that I should never have said as much while it remained a remote possibility.

'I saw the whole thing,' I went on. 'I think Seeley killed him, although I haven't any proof of that and I don't even know that he carries a gun.'

'He carries a gun all right,' said Orson, 'and I've got the bullet which killed the gamekeeper. If I can get hold of Seeley's gun, we can check up. Deane, anyone who knows about that murder is in danger. Miss Farring, myself, you . . .'

'I've realised that,' I said. 'I hope you've also realised that you've compromised yourselves hopelessly by burying the body. If the police find out about it they won't be easily convinced that you had nothing to do with the murder.'

'We were between the devil and the deep blue sea,' said Orson, bitterly. 'If we'd reported to the police, the Lord alone knows what would have happened!'

'What *are* you trying to tell me?' I demanded, with a

sudden flash of irritation. 'You're holding Farring prisoner, aren't you?'

'No,' said Orson.

'But . . .'

'We're keeping Farring at the other cottage so that he is available when certain people whom I don't know by name—or sight for that matter, except Seeley—can see him when they want to. They haven't been yet.' He looked at Elizabeth. 'Miss Farring, I think we ought to tell Deane what has happened, and what might come about, don't you?'

Elizabeth said: 'You said only an hour ago that at all costs he mustn't know!'

'We can't go on like this any longer,' said Orson. 'If there's a chance, we must take it.'

The issue was between the two of them, and I thought for a moment that Elizabeth was going to bring all her influence to bear against me. Then, abruptly, she said:

'Oh, tell him! It can't make it any worse!'

My heart jumped with elation, but I was surprised when Orson, after hesitating as if marshalling his thoughts, asked me abruptly whether I could walk. I said that I thought so.

'I'll lend you a hand,' he said.

I was not very steady on my legs, especially when we got to the head of a narrow staircase. The cottage was a large rambling place, filled with odd nooks and crannies. It was easy to imagine someone lurking in one of them.

We reached a door at the end of a narrow passage. This Orson flung open.

I stepped into a vast room. Such a great barn of a place was enough to fasten my interest in itself, but it was nothing compared with the contents.

I gaped about me, even my headache forgotten.

I have been through many picture galleries and museums in my time, and I had a fair idea of what the Arturo Collection would look like, but never had I seen such a one as this. The fact that pictures, vases, *objets d'art* and other treasures were standing cheek-by-jowl with no attempt at display or lighting could not rob them of their beauty. There must have been hundreds of different things in that room, from pictures which stood five or six feet high to miniatures and precious stones. In one corner stood a Grecian vase, nearly as tall as I; there were some sculptures which, in the poor light, seemed to have an unsurpassed beauty, a naturalness which took my breath away.

I said, slowly: 'So this is the Arturo Collection!'

Orson walked past me, looking round with an expression which I could not understand. Then he snapped his fingers and said abruptly:

'There isn't a genuine thing here, everything is faked!'

14

I Begin to Understand

'Everything!' I echoed.

'Every picture, every jewel, every piece of sculpture, every ornament—faked!' said Orson, bitterly. 'I ought to know, I've done most of the paintings myself, and I've helped with some of the other things.'

I did not trust myself to speak.

It was hard to believe even then; the bad light was one reason, of course, but everything had the illusion of perfection. I went to a picture hanging on the wall and looked at it, seeing the varnish was cracked and it looked dirty; every illusion had been carefully maintained. I picked up a small statuette which I could have sworn was silver. Orson took it from my hand and flung it to the floor. It broke into several pieces.

'Now perhaps you begin to understand,' he said, roughly.

I did not; I stared at him, trying to think clearly.

'For safety's sake the original collection was stored underground in the vaults of Sir Lancelot Bridie's country home,' said Orson. 'I do work for Farring, touching up, and painting copies when he doesn't want to put the originals on show. Some work was necessary on one or two less valuable pictures of the Arturo Collection, and I visited the vaults to do it; that is how I came to know that the collection was in England.'

'Where is it now?' I demanded.

'I don't know and Farring doesn't know,' said Orson, helplessly. 'That's why we've been stalling. We thought we would find out if we tried hard enough. The whole collection was removed in vans which were driven to the house by men whose credentials looked authentic enough to convince Bridie's secretary.'

'How long ago was this?' I asked.

'Nearly four years.'

'Four years! Then . . .'

'There has been plenty of time to look for it,' said Orson. 'Oh, I've seen it since it was stolen—not altogether, but items which had been provided so that I could make the copies. Other people, experts at their jobs, have made copies of everything else. Except for a "silver statuette",' he added with a savage note in his voice, 'this dummy collection is complete.'

'But why on earth do they want them copied?'

'I don't know,' said Orson. 'I've had orders and I've carried them out. You'll have guessed by now that I'm not a free agent, and nor is Farring.'

'What I can't understand is why the robbery wasn't reported as soon as it was discovered,' I said. 'There was nothing discreditable about having it in this country. All the regulations were observed, even Webb has admitted that.'

'Webb doesn't know everything,' said Orson, drily.

'Must you go into this?' Elizabeth asked. 'He'll only report to the police.'

'We've got to get something settled,' said Orson, 'and now that we've gone so far we'll go the whole hog. I suppose you realise, Miss Farring, that we might easily be suspected of murdering Abbott, and it would be extremely difficult to prove that we have not.'

I said: 'By doing what you've done without reporting to the police, you have made yourselves accessories. A report to me, in the circumstances, is as good as the police. You see, I can be helpful!'

I offered this small pleasantry in an effort to save our discussion—and so, Elizabeth—from becoming too lugubrious. I saw the point of Orson's comment, and knew that since Abbott's murder he was either seriously worried for himself or for the others.

'I hope to heaven we're not doing the wrong thing!' Elizabeth muttered.

'You're not,' I said. 'What doesn't Webb know, Orson?'

Orson said: 'All formalities and regulations were observed with a part of the collection, but secreted in the frames of some of the pictures and in other pieces were jewels and priceless old manuscripts which were brought into the country illegally—smuggled in, in plain words.'

'So your father . . . ?' I began, looking at Elizabeth.
'He knew nothing about it!'

'That's a tall story,' I said, not because I definitely disbelieved her, but because I thought I might pique her into talking more frankly.

She turned on me.

'It's the truth!' she cried fiercely. 'The arrangements were made before my father went to America to do some business on behalf of the Government. He knew nothing about the smuggled goods until after he returned. His manager had made the arrangements. My father could have gone to the police, then, I know— perhaps he should have done—but the goods were already sold and the money credited to his account. It was all done with fiendish cleverness, and it would have been almost impossible to prove his innocence. He thought it was done with, his own conscience was clear —and then, just after the collection was stolen, a man visited him.' She hesitated, and looked at Orson, who took up her story.

'Farring was visited by a man who knew what had happened and made it clear that Farring had no defence—he hadn't, of course; by keeping quiet he had tacitly admitted a share of the guilt. That's how it started. Farring had to do what he was told, or else be turned over to the police. Had that been the only thing, he would have faced it out,' went on Orson, 'but he wanted to get the collection back, and he thought he would have a chance of doing this if he pretended to play ball. He was asked to get me to work on making copies, and he thought that by doing that he would find out where the collection was and arrange somehow to get it back. He asked for my help, and that of one or two friends; and we agreed to do what we could. Every time a piece from the collection was released, however, it was carefully guarded, and we could never find out where it came from. Then we got deeper and deeper into the mire. I think the worry made Farring ill, and while he was in the nursing home I went to see him, and we agreed to make a clean breast of it. The very next day, he was taken away!'

'I see,' I said.

'You know pretty well everything that has happened since then,' said Orson. 'Forbes, the dealer, got hold of the Corot and knowing nothing about it offered it to Reccivi. You don't need telling any more why Farring has been avoiding Reccivi, do you?'

'A certain amount of persuasion was used, I suppose?'

'We were told that Reccivi must be stalled, and in view of everything that preceded it, that was done. Miss Farring knew nothing of this until I saw her.'

'You hadn't met her before?'

'Of course we hadn't met!' exclaimed Elizabeth. 'Do you think I would lie to you?'

I turned and looked at her.

'I wouldn't be surprised,' I said drily.

One big question was raised in my mind, but I did not try to get an answer to it then. There was one point which Orson might be able to resolve, and I went on: 'Exactly what is Farring doing here?'

'Waiting,' said Orson.

'For what?'

'For instructions,' said Orson bitterly. 'I don't know what part Seeley is playing.'

'Who is likely to give you instructions?'

'A man whom you have already seen, according to Miss Farring,' said Orson, 'flamboyantly disguised.'

'*That* merchant!' I exclaimed. 'I'd like to have another interview with him.'

100

'*You will have,*' a voice said.

My heart almost turned over as I recognised it on the instant. I saw Orson's eyes widen and felt sure that it was with alarm and that he had not seen the door open. Elizabeth gasped, and swung round.

The man with the false moustache and eyebrows stood on the threshold with an automatic in his hand. There was nothing striking about him, yet I always remember him as one of the most sinister individuals I have ever met.

He said: 'Deane, you were warned and you chose to ignore the warning. Orson, you will suffer for this.'

Orson drew in his breath.

'I probably will but . . .' He paused, and I thought the words that followed were as brave as any I have heard. 'You can count me on the other side. I'm through with appeasement.'

The man raised his gun.

Elizabeth forestalled him. With a lightening gesture she seized a small statuette and flung in with all her strength. It delayed the gunman and spoiled his aim. The bullet whizzed harmlessly through the air. I knew that the man had fired to kill and that he would do so again. There was a chance, and I took it. Perhaps I looked such a wreck that the man thought he had nothing to fear from me. He had swung round on Elizabeth and sent her flying with a back-hander, before levelling his gun again. He was only a couple of yards away from me and I covered the distance in two strides and then kicked at his arm. I scored a hit, getting his wrist. He did not loosen his hold on the gun, but his arm dropped. I steadied myself and rushed at him. He met me with a straight left which would have lifted me off my feet if it had caught me on the chin, but I swayed to one side, more by accident than design, and it just touched my neck. Then we collided. I was the heavier man and he was carried back, slipped and fell, striking his head on the floor.

The gun flew from his hand.

My head was hammering and I could hardly stand, but first and foremost I had to make sure that the man was out of action. The blow had dazed him but he was trying to get to his feet again. I clenched my fist, bent down, and cracked him under the jaw with a blow which finished him for the time being.

I don't know what happened in the next few seconds. When I was able to take notice again, the man with the disguise was still unconscious, and Orson was helping Elizabeth to her feet.

'You're sure you're all right?' he asked anxiously.

'Yes, of course.' She looked with horror at the man on the floor. Is he—dead?'

I said: 'If that killed him, he was in a pretty poor state.'

I picked up the gun, conscious of a sense of anti-climax which in different circumstances would have been funny. The man who had held the power of life and death over us for those few seconds was quite harmless now, and we stood looking at one another in that bizarre chamber of imitation wonders.

'Well, we can at least find out what he really looks like,' Orson said. He bent resolutely over the man and tugged gently at the moustache.

It did not move.

He pulled harder.

'It must be real!' exclaimed Orson.

'Nonsense,' I said, 'he must be using some special kind of gum.'

'It's *real*, I tell you,' said Orson.

Only then did I come to the conclusion that he was

right: the man's moustache and eyebrows were natural, while his hair had been dyed a lighter shade, adding to the bizarre effect.

We looked at him, baffled.

'What does it matter whether his eyebrows are his own or not!' demanded Elizabeth testily. 'The thing is, what are we going to *do* with him?'

'Why not keep him here?' I suggested, looking at Orson. 'Were you serious? Have you really come round on our side?'

He nodded, his expression solemn.

'Then I know exactly the man to keep you company for tonight,' I said, thinking of Anton. 'Elizabeth, will you telephone Downs House, and ask for . . . ?'

I stopped, for I realised that Anton might think it was a trick to get him out of the hotel, unless he recognised my voice. As the others watched me, I felt in a dilemma, for I did not want to leave them together with the unknown man. I suppose that at the time I did not really believe that Orson had swung round so completely.

'No, I'd better go,' I said. 'There's no hurry, anyhow. What about some rope, Orson?'

'What for?'

'To make sure he can't get away.'

'Isn't that rather melodramatic?' he asked.

'It was pretty melodramatic to shoot at you,' I said. 'If you're not certain whether it happened, have a look at the bullet hole in the wall. Have you some rope?'

Rather reluctantly he found a coil of picture cord and I spent five minutes making sure that our mystery man would have no freedom of movement when he came round. He was not badly hurt and I thought he showed signs of returning consciousness before I finished. I straightened up.

'That's that,' I said. 'Now show me the telephone.'

They both came with me, and as we retraced our steps through the house I was more conscious than ever of the dark alcoves and the unexpected nooks and crannies. Even the telephone cast a long, weird shadow on the pale wall behind it.

I lifted the receiver, but the exchange did not answer. The tension of the others increased as I kept on trying; but to all my efforts there was no response. As I replaced the receiver the silence was shattered by the clangorous ringing of the front-door bell.

15

Mr. Blundell in New Guise

In that gloomy hall, already on edge because of all that had happened, the three of us stared towards the door. None of us moved.

The bell rang again.

This time Orson relaxed, while I moved ahead of him, motioning him to one side. I did not think we had much to fear from whoever was there, otherwise he would not have announced his presence so boldly, but the last person I expected was Mr. Blundell. He stepped swiftly into the room, and I stifled a gasp of relief as I saw he was closely followed by Anton.

'Mr. Deane! Your head!' gasped Blundell. 'What has happened, sir, what has happened? I heard a shot. Your good friend here also heard it. We have been trying to find this house for the last twenty minutes!'

'It's all right, no one was hurt,' I said.

'Your head . . .'

'It's nothing,' I said sharply, 'and no one was hurt. I fired my gun by accident.'

I took out my automatic, and at the sight of it Blundell's eyes widened in alarm. I wondered why on earth Anton had not managed to sidetrack the man. Blundell was the last person in the world to trust with any secret, and if he even suspected the presence of a man upstairs, bound and gagged, he would go tearing to the police.

'Accident!' he exclaimed. 'Are you sure? My dear Miss Farring, are *you* hurt? You look pale. You were frightened, perhaps—Mr. Deane should have been more careful with a dangerous weapon. I suppose you know, Mr. Deane, that you require a licence for that gun?'

'I have one,' I said, tersely.

'Oh, indeed,' said Blundell, looking disappointed. 'I hope you will not make a practice of using it at night, it startled me very much.'

'It was silly of me,' I admitted, and made an effort to end the deadlock. 'Anton, you've arrived just in time to take Miss Farring back to the house. I think I ought to clean myself up a bit before I follow you, Mr. Orson has kindly offered to help me.'

Anton shot me a quick, sardonic smile.

'Now that we are here and there is nothing the matter I am hoping that Mr. Orson will let me look at his pictures,' he said.

Blundell broke in with an air of gallantry.

'In that case I will be charmed to escort Miss Farring back to the hotel, since I have already seen Mr. Orson's pictures and I know he will forgive me if I do not wait to see them again!' He smoothed down his waistcoat. 'Are you ready now, Miss Farring?'

I sympathised with Elizabeth. She wanted to know what we were going to do, but by refusing to go she would only make Blundell suspicious. She realised, too, that it was necessary to get the man out of the house. Orson looked about to make a protest, but bit his lip. His expression made me think again, and for the first time it occurred to me that Blundell might know more than he professed, and that in any case he might not be capable of saving Elizabeth if she were attacked by Seeley or anyone else.

Elizabeth moved graciously through the door, Blundell following.

Anton, to my surprise, closed the door on them quickly. Then he whispered:

'One of us must follow. Ned . . .'

'I'll go,' said Orson.

He gave us no opportunity to argue, but switched off the hall light, opened the door and went out.

'Can we trust that man?' demanded Anton.

'Blundell?'

'No, not that talkative fool! Orson.'

'I think we can,' I said.

'We will have to take a chance on it then,' said Anton. He switched on the light. 'I noticed that you appeared to be very friendly towards him. How did that come about? And how did you get that truly magnificent wound?'

'What on earth do I look like?' I demanded.

There was a mirror in the hall, and Anton led me to it.

As I surveyed my battered reflection, Anton said:

'My patience is nearly exhausted!'

'All right, I'll tell you,' I began, and then remembered the incident when Orson had first come into the sitting-room, before he had seen me. 'But wait a moment!' I hurried into the room and over to the bureau. I remembered exactly where his hands had been, and ran my fingers along the wood inside a small drawer. Nothing happened. I knew the tricks of secret hiding-places in old furniture, however.

Suddenly there was a sharp click.

Anton watched me with interest as I uncovered a cavity nearly half an inch wide. My explorative fingers touched something, and very gently I drew it out.

It was a wad of thin paper. I began to unfold it.

'How on earth did you know it was there?' Anton asked.

'I saw Orson trying to find it,' I said.

As I unfolded the paper—packed so tightly that it was almost solid—I gave him a brief outline of what had happened. I did not mention the fake collection; he would soon be able to see that for himself.

By the time I finished, there were only three folds left.

'When we've had a look at this we might be able to find out more of what the whole show is about,' I said.

Then I saw the door open.

I dropped my right hand to my pocket. I was too late to draw my gun, however, for the man facing me was armed. He was the man who I had confidently believed to be tied hand and foot, the man with the dark moustache and eyebrows!

He looked exactly the same, except that he had a bruise on his chin, where I had hit him. The expression in his eyes was such that I was quite sure that he was prepared to shoot, and when he did so he would shoot to kill.

Another man came from behind him. What a fool I had been! What a fool! I should have suspected that he had a colleague in the house. Obviously the second man had released him. These thoughts flashed through my mind as I stared at the automatic.

His companion, a little fellow with a blank face and nothing remarkable about him, came forward and took the paper out of my hand.

I said nothing. Anton gave me the impression that he was going to jump forward, and I hoped that he would not, although I was prepared to back him up if he did. I had managed to get away with such an attack once, but did not think my luck would hold a second time.

'Stay still, Duval,' said the gunman, 'I do not want to have to shoot you.'

'You've changed,' I said.

'I advise you not to attempt to sharpen your not very bright wits on me,' he retorted. 'You have already got yourself into considerable trouble. However, this time I want to help you.'

I stared at him, my strongest feeling one of relief that he had not yet fired his gun.

'Orson has completely fooled you,' he said. 'But for the one statuette that collection is genuine. It is worth a fortune, and he and Farring are trying to make sure that they get possession of it. You have been deceived by Farring as well as by Orson, and if you are wise you will not take his daughter on trust.'

'I don't believe you,' I said.

The other shrugged.

'Go upstairs and see for yourself. I believe you know a little about old things, and you should be able to make sure from one or two of the pieces. I have all I want,' he added, taking the paper from his companion. 'Take my advice, Deane, and get out of this business before it is too late.'

He backed to the door, still covering us with his gun.

The little man went out first. I heard the front door open, and close.

Anton leapt after them, but before he reached the hall both men had gone.

'Don't open it!' I warned him.

He ignored me, and opened the door. A bullet smashed into a table just behind him.

'Why must you take chances like that?' I demanded. 'They were bound to shoot if you attempted to follow them.'

'Yes. I was wrong,' said Anton unrepentantly, 'but, Ned, why did he leave you here? You said that he was determined to kill all of you upstairs. And what is this talk of the collection?'

'He's had time to think,' I said, 'and now he thinks it's a good idea to make us doubtful about Orson.'

'Weren't you doubtful all the time?'

I shrugged.

'The collection!' Anton almost howled. 'What of that?'

I told him what I knew about it as we went upstairs. Oddly enough, I was no longer affected by the shadowed gloom; perhaps I felt sure that now the two men who had been lurking there had gone, there was nothing else for me to worry about. I found the big barn of a room without any trouble, and switched on the light. Just before I did so I had a wild thought that something might have happened in there, that the contents might have been moved away; it was absurd, because it would have taken half a dozen men all day to move it.

Everything was there just as when I had left the room.

Anton stood looking round, in amazement. I picked up one of the pictures, an Italian pastoral scene, at least three centuries old—if it were genuine.

'Can all these be fakes?' asked Anton, in a marvelling voice.

'They *could* be,' I said, 'and I'd rather believe Orson than the other merchant. Orson ought to be back before long, unless he went further than the door of the hotel. And that reminds me, where did you leave Sheila?'

'In her room, under oath not to leave it,' said Anton.

'You took your time,' I said.

Anton grimaced.

'I heard someone in the grounds and followed him. It turned out to be Blundell! It would have been difficult to do anything else.'

I said worriedly: 'I hope *he's* not in this.'

'You're in a mood to suspect anyone,' said Anton, 'even that block of ice, the receptionist.'

'You went a fair way to melt her,' I said, and then added in exasperation: 'Why on earth are we standing here talking drivel? We've enough to think about without wasting time on Blundell and the receptionist!'

It was nearly eleven o'clock before Orson came in.

He told us that he had seen Elizabeth and Blundell safely to Downs House, and then had gone to see Farring to make sure that the older man was all right. The art dealer was at the cottage with his 'warder', a useful fellow, according to Orson, who would not be afraid to use a gun if he or Farring were attacked.

The explanation was reasonable enough, and I accepted it.

Then I broke the news about the unknown man's return and the theft of the paper. I made no bones about admitting that I had taken it out of the bureau, but I did not mention that the collection had been called genuine.

I watched Orson closely.

110

The loss of the paper was obviously a blow to him.

He did not speak immediately, and Anton and I suppressed our impatience with difficulty.

At last, he said: 'Now we *are* completely in their hands!' When neither of us spoke, he went on with an obvious effort: 'That paper was a list of all the goods which were smuggled into England with the Arturo Collection, in Farring's own handwriting. He made it out when he first heard what had happened.'

'Why on earth did he do a thing like that?' I demanded.

'He thought it was necessary,' said Orson. 'Look here, Deane, this has been a remarkable business from first to last. I don't know how well you know Farring.'

'Only by repute,' I said.

'Well, his reputation, up to this affair, will stand up to any inquiry,' said Orson, 'and he was determined to try to find every smuggled item of the goods and return it to the collection. On the list were those items which he had been able ro retrieve.'

'Where did he put the smuggled goods?'

'With the collection.'

'So those he had got back were stolen, too.'

'Yes, I'm afraid so,' said Orson, and then he added with a rather tired smile: 'Of course I do see that much of this must sound nonsense to you, and I can only tell you what I know. Farring has kept some things from me. All I know about Farring, today, is that he is determined to stay here until he receives further "instructions", and that he has been frightened out of all idea of reporting to the police. I can't help feeling that he knows something which he hasn't divulged, and that these people have used some means of persuasion which has not only made him await their commands, but

111

which has cast him into the depths of despair. It's heartbreaking to see him!'

That did more than anything else to convince me of Orson's sincerity; his words reminded me so vividly of the way Farring had looked.

I did not feel that I could do anything more that night; in fact I would not be in any shape for anything until I had slept. I agreed that it was a good idea when Anton said that he would stay with Orson, but he accompanied me halfway to Downs House, from which point I insisted on completing the journey by myself.

Sheila and Elizabeth were in their room, and I must have looked all in, for Elizabeth refrained from asking questions. I simply told them what Anton was doing, and went into my own room, after exacting a promise from Sheila that she would bolt her door and keep the window closed all night.

I was in bed and asleep within five minutes.

I suppose it was the effect of the headache, the tablets which I had taken and the general excitement. There have been times when I would have been horrified at the idea of going off to sleep so soundly at such a time, but I did not give it a second thought that night.

It was bright and sunny when I woke up. My head was better, but still painful at a sudden movement. I glanced at my watch and was amazed to see it was nearly eleven o'clock.

'Eleven!' I exclaimed, and flung the clothes back.

Then there was a tap at the door and Sheila appeared, looking fresh and lovely.

'There's nothing you can do today,' she said, 'you're in no state to go round looking for trouble, darling, so I've arranged for breakfast in bed.'

'I'm not having any breakfast in bed,' I said, firmly, a cup of tea will do me until lunch-time, and whether you

112

like it or not I'm getting up!'

Five minutes later I was facing a lightly boiled egg, toast and marmalade on a tray, my pillows banked up behind me. I was determined to get up for lunch, however, but just after twelve Sheila and Anton came in, Anton grinning all over his face because he had come in about three o'clock, slept on the divan placed in my room, and got up again at eight, without disturbing me.

'I thought you were on duty with Orson,' I said.

'Cris telephoned and asked me to leave him there alone,' said Anton. 'Ned,' he added darkly, 'Cris is up to something!'

'Where is he?' I demanded.

'I don't know. He telephoned—so you see the telephone service to Orson's house was restored—and I did what he asked. I didn't see him, and I haven't seen him this morning, although I went to the village and asked for Mr. Carey.'

'Was he there?' I asked.

'No, he had not been there during the night. He looked in about ten o'clock, and left without saying where he was going.'

'Now what *is* this?' I demanded. 'That's enough mystery without Cris making it worse. Why doesn't he show himself?'

'I don't know,' said Anton, soberly. He sat on the edge of the bed, and added: 'I do know one thing, Ned. Mr. Carey will never be recognised as Sheila's brother. The description which the old man at the inn gave me was very different from Cris.'

'So he's up to his old tricks again,' I said with a groan.

A wizard at disguise, he had obviously foreseen the disadvantage of his likeness to Sheila. I was glad about this, but I could not see what point there was in making a mystery as far as Anton and I were concerned.

All day I expected him to telephone, but there was no message from him.

It was a curious day. There was so much on my mind, and so much which might happen—but did not. A day's rest was important for me, yet I was impatient and worried. The situation was so involved that I felt justified in keeping the gamekeeper's murder to myself, and in any case I believed that if it were disclosed, the local police would come, disinter the body, and put the house and grounds under guard. That would serve no purpose except to warn off the two men who had left with the paper from Orson's bureau, and I felt that Webb would be far from pleased to have the local police brought in while the affair was at its present stage.

I was uneasy about Farring's position.

There was one obvious weakness in Orson's story, and the weakness was in Farring's behaviour. If the story were true, then Farring had some very strong reason for behaving as he did, some guilty secret greater than any to which he had admitted, and about which Orson might know nothing.

I was worried by Orson. The suggestion that he had lied about the collection I had seen, kept coming back to my mind. It was possible that the studio contained the real Arturo Collection, and yet, if that were so, I could not imagine that Orson would leave it there, and tell me about it. After all, he had no assurance that I would not go back on my word and inform the police.

It seemed to me a pointless day, and I was not surprised that Orson spent a lot of it with Elizabeth. She appeared to have resigned herself to waiting until someone else forced the issue, and she contributed little to the admittedly aimless discussions in which the rest of us indulged. I thought Orson was extremely considerate of her comfort, and it crossed my mind that they might have lied, and were in fact old friends. He gave me the impression that he was in love with her, and trying to avoid showing it.

About Blundell, too, I was far from happy.

He was about the hotel much less than he had been the previous evening, and I could not help feeling that there was something furtive in his manner. Moreover, he seemed different. I put that down to the fact that I was getting to know him better, but I was surprised at the way in which he kept in the background. Point was given to my uneasiness when I heard one of the residents say to his wife:

'Blundell isn't making such a nuisance of himself today as he usually does. I hear he's going to London tomorrow.'

'Keep your fingers crossed, dear,' said his wife.

If Blundell's manner was sufficiently altered to make regular guests notice it, I was right.

Sheila was with me most of that day and the next. Blundell did go to London; or at least, he left to catch a London train.

I was feeling much better by then, and even more impatient at doing nothing. I said as much to Orson, who looked at me grimly.

'Now you know what this interminable waiting is like! One never knows what might happen next.' He broke off abruptly. 'I suppose the truth is that I'm scared stiff.'

I liked him for that frank admission.

I went to bed reasonably early, we all did, while Orson returned soon after dinner to his cottage.

It must have been a couple of hours after I had got to sleep when I was awakened by a frantic banging on the door. I jumped out of bed, but Anton was too quick for me, and pulled the door open. It was Elizabeth.

'It's on fire!' she gasped. 'It's on fire!'

I thought she meant Farring's cottage, and said: 'Your father ...'

'No, Orson's place,' she said. 'It's burning furiously, and he's still there!'

16

Another Question Unanswered

The fire was an awe-inspiring spectacle. I know that the words are trite, but it was exactly that.

I had pulled on my trousers and put on an overcoat, Anton did the same, and both girls appeared in sweaters and slacks. Others in the hotel had been disturbed and there was an excited party in the hall. Some of the men had already gone to help, but I gathered that there was not much hope of saving the cottage. There was no water near, except from a well, which carried barely enough for household needs.

I did not see Blundell, and assumed that he had gone with the other men.

Outside, the sky was like burnished gold. Now and again a tongue of flame shot up above the tops of the trees, like a fiery demon seeking its freedom. It was warm as we drew near the scene, with Elizabeth a few paces ahead of us. Her anxiety for Orson was so obvious that I found it increasingly difficult to believe that she could feel so keenly for a man who was a comparative stranger, and one moreover whom she had reason to distrust.

The heat was now almost unbearable, blown forward by the fire which had evidently started in the back of the house. I heard the crash of falling masonry, and thought that part of the roof had caved in.

Elizabeth was like a crazed thing, and twice Anton had to restrain her from plunging into the flames, for the stairs were already ablaze. We were told that a man had gone to save Orson, but there was little likelihood that either of them would get out. Elizabeth raved and shouted at us, calling us cowards and fools, but no man would have been justified in going into that burning mass.

There was one corner where we might be luckier, and Anton and I, with two other men, went towards it. Here a ladder was propped crazily against a window sill. Somewhat gingerly, and with little liking for the part of hero, I began to climb. Elizabeth's voice urging me on came at the start, but soon the only sound I could hear was the roaring fire.

I got into a room without any trouble. Beyond was a narrow passage, at the end of which I could see the flames.

I reached the door, and then, through the billowing smoke, I saw the bodies of two men. One was Orson, but I did not recognise the other. His clothes were smouldering and might burst into flames at any moment, and he lay on his face. Orson was on his back, unconscious.

I began to drag the unknown man towards the window, without much hope that I could get them both to safety before the floor collapsed. Nor would I have done so but for Anton who came from behind me and seized hold of Orson.

117

Another man, quick-witted and capable, stretched out eager hands from the top of the ladder. In an incredibly short time we were all outside and in comparative safety.

In the light of the fire behind me, I saw the face of Orson's companion, and I have never been more astonished: it was *Blundell*!

He was coming round.

There are moments which stand out vividly in every man's life, I suppose, and none stands out in my memory more clearly than that moment, when Blundell opened his eyes.

Anton nudged me; he, too, had recognised the man.

I tried to speak; then the wind brought an eddy of smoke, and I coughed violently.

'There's no one else in there, is there?' someone asked anxiously.

'I don't think so. Orson will know.'

Orson was sitting up, conscious but dazed. Blundell, whose smouldering clothes had been doused with a bucket of water, was protesting that he was all right. I think the respect which everyone felt for Blundell that night was enough to give added tension to the atmosphere; no one had dreamed the man capable of it.

Orson's eyes sought out and held those of Elizabeth. I sensed her enormous relief at his safety, and thought grimly of the way she had denied knowing him; confound it, she was in love with the man, and he with her!

This was no time for asking questions, however.

Soon police and firemen arrived from Menlow, but they could do very little. I suppose my own exertions made me temporarily forgetful of all that had been destroyed in the fire, for I gave it little thought.

So many people were near Blundell that I did not go to him. The others were less embarrassed than I at the

118

way we had all misjudged him. They wanted to carry him, but he insisted on walking back to the hotel.

I heard the story from someone else. Blundell had been one of the first to see the fire, it appeared, and had raised the alarm and gone hurrying over to the house. Only one other man, a servant, had seen him rush through the front door and up the stairs.

Two things emerged in my mind; first, that Blundell had been so prompt, and second, that he must have known Orson's room and been familiar with the twisting passages of the house. It was a point to remember next day, when Blundell would undoubtedly be the hero of the hour. If he reacted in character, he would probably be unbearable. It was ungenerous to think this, but in spite of all that had happened, I could not bring myself to like the man.

It was four o'clock before we got back to bed. Tired though I was, my chief worry was the possibility that the collection had been genuine. The thought of such treasures going up in smoke was a nightmare, though not one acute enough to keep me awake.

Everyone was late next morning.

Just before luncheon, I was called to the telephone. It was a long-distance call, and I was not surprised to hear Webb's voice. As he asked me at once what sort of holiday I had had, I understood he did not wish me to mention that he was a member of the police force.

'Oh, I can't grumble,' I said, 'there's plenty to do.'

'I rather thought I'd come down to Salisbury tomorrow, and if you can meet me I'd be glad,' he said. 'Let's make it lunch, shall we?'

'Right. What time, and where?'

'One o'clock at the Grange Hotel.'

I rang off, satisfied and rather glad that he had given me good notice. I could talk about it with the others, and perhaps Cris would turn up and we could get his opinion. I lunched at a table with Sheila, Elizabeth and Orson, and would have enjoyed it but for a conversation which started at the next table.

A woman was speaking, and her voice carried clearly to us.

'One thing's very certain, I shan't feel safe going along *that* road again.'

'Nonsense, my dear!'

'It isn't nonsense, Fred, and I don't care what you say. He *must* have been murdered.'

'Don't be absurd,' said her husband, 'he was probably knocked down by a car, and the driver didn't report it. They'll get the man, though, there's no need to worry about that. Now don't be morbid, Lucy, just because you happened to hear about it in the village, there's no need to spoil your lunch.'

'*Your* lunch is all you're worried about,' said Lucy.

I did not like that talk at all; dead bodies found in the vicinity of Downs House were liable to cause awkward complications, and coming on top of the fire, might bring the Salisbury police here in strength. The finishing touch was put to my uneasiness when a woman, who had overheard the conversation, joined in.

'They say they don't know who it is, but it's a funny thing. Jim Abbott hasn't been seen since the night before last, and if the clothes that dead man was wearing weren't his, *I'll* be surprised!'

Sheila noticed nothing, but I knew that Abbott was the name of the gamekeeper, whose disappearance would soon become a topic of conversation in Menlow. The mention of the clothes worried me, too. I knew that we had taken Orson's word for the fact that the gamekeeper had been buried—true, I had jumped to that

thing had gone wrong in the kitchen, and there was much murmuring and muttering about it. I hurried upstairs afterwards, for some old trousers, and, a little before nine o'clock, Anton, Orson and I went to Farring's cottage. Orson got a couple of spades from a gardener's shed, and we set to work in the darkness, only occasionally showing a torch. It was drizzling a little and the soil clung to our shoes, and in spite of the work it was unpleasantly cold.

It was in fact one of the most unpleasant jobs I have ever tackled, although common sense told me that if Abbott's body was not there, the grave would be empty. Then my spade struck something other than the soil. I stopped, and my heart turned over. We worked on more carefully, until, finally, we knew for certain that we were coming upon the body of a man.

Anton shone the torch on the face, and I stared down incredulously.

Orson exclaimed aloud: 'It's Blundell!'

'But Blundell was at dinner!' protested Anton.

Only then did the meaning of Blundell's altered manner and appearance dawn on me. The Blundell who had rescued Orson was an impostor.

17

I Interview 'Mr. Blundell'

'What are we going to do?' whispered Orson.

'Leave him here,' said Anton.

'We'd better do that for the time being,' I said, 'but we'll make quite sure that he's dead, first.'

It was a ghoulish thought but I refused to be satisfied until I had made sure that there was no possibility of the man being buried alive. Then we put the earth back. I liked the job even less than that of uncovering it, but for the time being I felt sure that there was nothing else we could do. It took us over an hour before we finished, and then when the torch's flare shone on each of us in turn, we saw what a mess we were in.

Orson suggested that we should go to Farring's cottage and clean ourselves up. I agreed, and in the few minutes which it took us to walk to the cottage, I did some high-powered thinking. It seemed likely that someone had discovered that Blundell had got wind of the affair, had then killed him and seen an excellent chance of taking his place. Blundell was a man whom no one really looked at, because they were always on edge to get away from him, and a good disguise would succeed in his case where it would fail with most people. He had kept himself out of the way for two days, and the only time he had taken any risk was when he had rescued Orson; that was certainly a point in his favour, but it seemed to me that there were people who did not want either Orson or Farring dead.

I reached one decision. We had taken enough chances with Farring. When we had cleaned ourselves up a little, I looked at Anton and said firmly:

'One of us is going to stay here with Farring, whether he likes it or not.'

'And you want me to stay,' said Anton, drily

'Will you mind?'

'I would not rob you of the opportunity of interviewing the second Mr. Blundell for the world, Ned! Go on, and accuse him!'

Orson said: 'I'm sure they won't do Farring any

serious injury. He—he's doing what they want him to, and that's the way they want it.'

'We'll have it our way,' I said. 'You know, Orson, this business can't go on much longer. Either things have got to come to a head, or else the police will have to be formally advised. This is the second murder in these grounds within forty-eight hours.'

Orson raised no further objection. The 'warder'—whom Orson assured me was an old associate of Farring's—was informed, and he begged us not to tell Mr. Farring; apart from that, I think, he was relieved at the prospect of having company. We left Anton comfortably installed in an easy chair in the study, and went back to Downs House, having arranged for Orson to relieve Anton later. Elizabeth and Sheila were in the lounge. Orson went to join them, and I went straight up to Blundell's room.

He called out 'Come in'.

When I got inside and saw him, sitting in a dressing-gown in front of an electric fire, I could have sworn it was the man whom I had seen the first night, but soon I realised that the eyes were not the same, and seeing him for the first time in a good light and at close quarters I saw other things which gave away the fact that he was disguised.

'Why, Mr. Deane!' he exclaimed. 'I'm delighted to see you, delighted! Do come in, my dear fellow, do come in!'

'I thought I would have a look at that caricature which you mentioned,' I said, 'as well as inquire after your health.'

'Delighted, delighted!' said Blundell, and now I knew that his voice was higher-pitched than that of the man I had first heard. 'Er—caricature, now.'

'You told me about it the first night I was here,' I said.

'Oh, to be sure!' He beamed at me. 'You know, Deane, it's been rather unusual. I haven't had an experience like I had the night before last ever before! When I think of it, I shudder! Those flames . . .'

'I haven't congratulated you yet,' I said.

'Oh, my dear fellow, please!'

There was a pause, and then I said lightly: 'And the caricature?'

He waved his hand towards a crayon drawing hanging on the wall by the side of the fireplace.

It was a good caricature, bold, clear, showing up Blundell's heavy features well. I looked at it, and I looked at the man sitting opposite me.

'Not bad, not bad at all. Now tell me who you are.'

'My dear sir!'

I said: 'The body of the man you're supposed to be has been found.'

That had him! He rose from his chair, his likeness to Blundell subtly altering.

'My God, Ned, that's bad!' he said.

The voice, the 'Ned', the way he spoke, told me who he was, and yet I stared at him with my mouth agape, unable to believe it. '*By God, Ned, that's bad!*' uttered in a voice with which I was as familiar as my own; *this was Cris!*

My stupefaction must have amused him, for he grinned and put a hand on my arm.

'Come! It isn't as bad as that!'

'You—you—you *devil*!' I said, weakly, and sat down.

I had come into the room filled with the determination to force a showdown with 'Blundell', calculating what I should say and how I should handle the situation to a nicety. I had been confident, too; and now I felt like a punctured balloon. As I sat there looking at him and trying to regain my composure, I realised that there had been plenty of indications. This man was disguised, and Cris was a genius at the art; he had not stayed at the inn in Menlow, yet obviously he had been in the district.

'How long would you have kept it up?' I demanded.

'You would have seen through it before long,' he said. 'Tell me, Ned, are you sure about Blundell?'

'Yes, I've just seen his body.'

'Then I've been living in a fool's paradise,' said Cris, 'and a very pretty scheme has gone awry.'

'I haven't cottoned on to this business yet,' I said. 'How on earth did you manage to get here so quickly?' Before he answered, I went on : 'Was it you at Orson's house the other night, when you came with Anton?'

'Yes. I'd just arrived.'

'If Anton knew . . .' I began.

'I think he suspected it,' said Cris, 'but I'm not sure. It doesn't matter a tinker's curse, anyhow. I got here quickly because Clyde asked me to; he sent for me from France and gave me an idea of what was afoot. As it happens, he and Blundell are old acquaintances, Blundell having once been in the Foreign Office. Clyde telephoned Blundell and asked him to go to London, and put the position to him—would he mind being impersonated for a few days. Blundell didn't mind. He came back to collect a few personal belongings and was going to London until I sent him the all clear. Poor beggar!' added Cris. 'He must have walked into trouble as soon as he left here and before I took his place. How was he killed?'

'I don't know,' I said, and told Cris what I had seen. Then : 'Did he know anything at all?' I asked.

'Nothing about this business.'

It was clear to us both that someone had known of the intended impersonation, and killed the real Blundell thinking him to be Cris. The only alternative was that Blundell had stumbled across something in his last few hours at Downs House, and I did not think that was likely.

'Well, we're in a mess now,' I said, 'but I suppose we'll get through it somehow.' I paused for a moment and then demanded: 'Why did Clyde send for you? I was under the impression that I had struck something by accident. Why the dickens didn't he tell me if it was a departmental business!'

'It isn't.'

'But he sent for you and Anton . . .'

'At the urgent request of Scotland Yard,' said Cris. He turned to the dressing-table and began to remove his make-up.

As he wiped the greasepaint off, he told me the position as far as he knew it. There were few new facts, but for the first time I learned how the affair was viewed by Scotland Yard and the Home Office.

Cris had been clearing up odds and ends of a chase in France when Clyde had recalled him by telephone. Directly he had arrived in London, the day after Sheila and I reached Menlow, he had seen Clyde and Superintendent Webb. Both of them had made it clear that he was under no obligation to take part in this affair, but Webb outlined the situation and told him what I was doing and that Anton had already come down.

'Clyde knew perfectly well that you would come like a shot,' I said.

'I suppose so,' admitted Cris. 'Actually I hadn't a great deal of choice, seeing that you three were already deeply involved, but even without that I would have been interested. The Arturo Collection is no small thing, the behaviour of Farring is puzzling . . .'

'Do they know where he is?' I asked.

'Oh yes. Didn't Webb tell you?'

'No, but I'll tell him a thing or two when I see him next,' I said grimly.

'On the whole I think he was wise,' said Cris. 'He wanted you to come down and try to find out things for yourself, and he thought it better if you weren't fore-warned. At least, that's what I assume.'

'He wanted to make sure that if I were questioned I couldn't give away the fact that the police knew Far-ring was here,' I said.

Cris smiled.

'Have it your own way! I suppose if they kept you in the dark as much as that, they didn't tell you why they've let Farring stay down here, and why they've preferred to work through us and in secret.'

'They certainly omitted that little courtesy,' I said drily.

'My, my, you do feel badly about it! As a matter of fact we have been highly honoured, Ned! Scotland Yard has entrusted us with an inquiry which they feel is too delicate for themselves to handle. They think that the Arturo Collection has been stolen, although they're not sure of it. The collection of old masters, art treasures and jewels,' went on Cris, 'is one which affects the most unlikely personages, some of whom are scrupulously honest and highly respectable in all other directions but appear to consider that such treasures are fair game. On this occasion, items known to belong to the Arturo Collection have been discovered in the possession of no less a person than a member of the British Cabinet.'

'Great Scott!' I exclaimed. 'Who?'

'You'd hardly expect Webb to tell us that,' said Cris. 'I think Clyde knows, but is under an oath of secrecy. It is highly embarrassing matter for Scotland Yard and for the Home Office! The Yard is working on it, of course, but hasn't got much forrader. Farring himself has been questioned, but makes no admissions, and until the murder of the art dealer in Chelsea, and the attack on Reccivi, no apparent crime had been committed. I'll tell you one thing,' he added. 'Since the murder, the pace has speeded up. If we can't see the business through in a couple of days, the Yard will be forced to come into the open, with all the ensuing consequence of trouble and scandal.'

'You can add two more murders to the art dealer's,' I said drily.

'*Two?*'

I told him about Abbott, and the rather curious relationship between Elizabeth and Orson, expressing my opinion that they were old acquaintances. Finally I admitted that I could make neither head nor tale of it; the destruction of the dummy—or possibly real—collection had turned the whole business into a crazy affair which no one in their right senses could understand.

'Hm!' said Cris, when I had finished.

There was a tap at the door, followed by Sheila and Anton.

I looked up, grinning, as I saw them step towards Cris, who had his back towards them.

He turned suddenly.

'Cris!' cried Sheila. 'Cris!'

She flung herself into his arms, while Anton stared at him in a stupefaction which matched my own, until finally he uttered the same words as I had done.

'You *devil*, Cris!'

No one who had not been one of our small company can really understand how we felt. Since I had realised who 'Blundell' was, I had been much happier; it was as if a heavy weight had been lifted from my shoulders. Even my annoyance at the high-handed behaviour of Webb, and what I considered to be the needless discretion of Clyde, were superficial things. Not only were we all three working together again, but there were signs that at last Cris had succeeded in ridding himself of the worst shadows which had fallen across him with the death of his fiancée.

I bolted the door, as a precaution, and then Cris gave the others an outline of the situation. Anton seemed more affected than I thought he would be.

'I don't like it, Cris. It is unpleasantly reminiscent of the kind of thing that happened in France before the collapse. The protection of highly placed politicians . . .'

'Stuff and nonsense,' said Cris, gaily. 'If this great man is implicated, then it will come out and there'll be no hushing up. All the authorities want to do is to make sure that before they come out in the open, they know the whole truth. They might not find it if they acted too precipitately. Supposing they arrested Farring, Orson, Elizabeth and anyone else they can lay their hands on. It's not by any means sure that they would get to the bottom of the business. They're doing it the best way—if they thought a different one would get results more quickly, they would use it.'

'I hope you are right,' said Anton.

I knew a lot about the treachery and chicanery in French political circles before the war, and was not surprised that Anton felt as he did. He was amenable enough, however.

We then switched to the plan of campaign.

Over this, I admitted, I was getting a little worried.

I did not see that we were any further ahead than we had been at the start. Three men had been murdered and Orson's house with all its contents destroyed. There was still nothing to suggest the real reason for Farring's behaviour, although the sum total of all we knew, especially the written list of smuggled goods, might be good enough reason for it. I was not convinced of that, however.

Finally, I said: 'The only man whom we feel pretty sure is involved is Seeley. The others remain as mysterious as ever. I for one am tired of waiting for them to make the first move, and I suggest that we tackle Seeley next.'

Cris shrugged his shoulders.

'Tackle Seeley, then, but be careful in doing it. I haven't yet met the gentleman,' he added. 'Supposing one of you take me along?'

It was decided that Anton should do that, while Sheila and I went in search of Elizabeth.

I expected to find her in the double room, but she was not there.

'She seems to prefer your room,' said Sheila, mischievously.

We tapped next door, but there was no answer. After a second tap, I attempted to open it; but it was locked.

'Elizabeth!' I called, urgently. 'It's Ned—open the door!'

There was still no answer, and Sheila was now as anxious as I was. I took out my penknife, and picked the lock. I heard it go back, but when I tried to open the door it did not move, and I knew that it was bolted.

'What's wrong?' called a voice from along the passage, and, turning, I saw Cris coming towards us.

Later I learned that Seeley had not been in his room,

but for the moment I had completely forgotten Seeley as I hurried down the stairs. Anton joined me.

'Elizabeth's bolted herself in,' I said tersely.

Although it was dark outside, we had no difficulty in locating our rooms. A tree grew near the wall, and Anton, more agile than I, swung himself to a low bough and then to another, while I waited below, shining a torch so that it reflected on the window.

It was open.

Anton's figure disappeared from view, and a moment later the light in the room was switched on. I heard nothing, and, unable to restrain myself any longer, I climbed up after him.

The room was not disturbed, but Elizabeth lay on the bed, with her eyes closed. A stocking appeared to be tied tightly about her neck, and this Anton was furiously cutting.

18

Another Attempt at Murder

As I lowered myself into the room, and turned by force of habit to draw the curtains, I felt sick.

When I turned back, the stocking was loose, and Sheila was bending over Elizabeth.

Cris said: 'Up to you, Ned.'

He was feeling her pulse, and from his grave face I judged that he could detect no beating. I know more about first-aid than the others, and when Elizabeth had been lifted to the floor I knelt over her and began to administer artificial respiration.

The marks of the stocking about her neck stood out like ridges, and her throat, usually so slender and pale, was red and swollen.

I said sharply: 'Telephone a doctor, and tell him that we'll need oxygen.'

Sheila nodded and slipped out of the room.

I worked on steadily, but there was no alteration in Elizabeth's colour and no suggestion that she would come round. After ten minutes, Anton relieved me, then Cris relieved him, and I started again.

Halfway through my second spell, I thought there was a contraction of her throat muscles. I would not stop even for the few seconds necessary for one of the others to take over. My head was swimming, and I began to ache in every limb, but I worked as I have never done before.

Suddenly, Elizabeth's body shivered; I could feel the movement under my hands. I spent another half-minute or so, and then let Anton take over. I stood gasping for breath, streaming with sweat as I watched Elizabeth's face for the tell-tale signs of returning life.

Anton was nearly as much a wreck as I when he finished, but before he did so, we knew that the thousandth chance had come off. I was too tired to feel elated, but was conscious of a deep satisfaction when Elizabeth drew in a quick breath. It would be some time before she was back to normal, but there was now no need to work with the same frenzy.

I took over again.

Only then did I realise that Sheila had not returned. It was now nearly an hour since she had left to telephone. I looked up at the door, and then said to Anton:

'Where's Cris?'

'He'll be back,' said Anton.

'Did Sheila come in?'

'I'm not sure.'

What could have gone wrong? Sheila should be back. I was on edge, but suddenly the door opened and Cris appeared.

I said sharply: 'Where's Sheila?'

'The doctor won't be long,' said Cris quietly.

'Never mind the doctor! Where's Sheila?'

'I don't know,' said Cris. 'Ned, you stay here and look after Elizabeth, Anton and I will look for Sheila.'

I suppose that was wise, for I was more tired than the others, and in no shape to go out and start looking for anyone, but I came near to hating them as they quickly left me. Here was I, forced to stay with Elizabeth, while Sheila was missing. I worked on steadily, because it was the only thing I could do.

The doctor arrived in ten minutes. He had an oxygen cylinder with him and all the necessary equipment, and he took over at once. I did not question him at first, but as he finished getting things ready and the oxygen was being pumped gently into Elizabeth, I said:

'Who telephoned you?'

'A lady,' said the doctor. He was a middle-aged man whom I had seen at the hotel once before. 'You've done a pretty good job already. How did this happen?'

I mumbled something unintelligible and left him to it. I washed my hands and plunged my face under water. Obviously Sheila had telephoned the doctor, and then gone off somewhere else; I could only imagine that she had been waylaid.

'She'll be all right,' the doctor said, after what seemed a long time. He looked at me curiously. 'This should be reported, you know.'

I pulled myself together, and said that as it had ended so well, I hoped that he would not think it necessary.

I saw that he was by no means happy about it, and at last said in some exasperation:

'All right, report it if you must, but to Scotland Yard, not to the local police!'

He looked startled.

'I don't quite understand you.'

'Of course you don't,' I said. 'I'm sorry, but this has affected me rather badly. If you care to telephone Scotland Yard, in confidence, I'm sure that they will satisfy you that you've done the right thing. It mustn't be known in the hotel that I have any connection with the Yard, of course.'

'I see,' he said, slowly. 'All right, sir, I will do that.'

As a matter of fact, he didn't; presumably he thought that I spoke of Scotland Yard with sufficient authority, and in any case there was nothing serious in failing to make a report.

When the door closed on him I felt terribly lonely.

I could not leave the room very well, for whoever had tried to murder Elizabeth might come back, but I wished more than ever that I had made some kind of attempt to go with Cris, leaving Anton here. My mind was filled with stark forebodings. I pictured Sheila lying in the grounds with a rope round her neck; shot; run over by the car which had been used to disfigure Abbott the gamekeeper.

I kept the door ajar, and looked out several times, and when I heard footsteps which I thought were Anton's, I reached the door in a couple of strides and flung it open, to the obvious surprise of one of the hotel residents.

'Oh,' I said, acutely disappointed.

'Good evening, Mr. Deane,' he said. 'Your friend telephoned and asked me to give you a message. He said that there is nothing at all to worry about.'

136

He looked at me curiously, so I tried to pull myself together, thanked him, and was heartily glad when he went off again.

'There is nothing to worry about,' I repeated to myself.

I was prey to doubts, however, even after that. Suppose the message had not come from Cris or Anton? But just after eleven o'clock I heard footsteps and voices. This time I was more composed as I opened the door.

Cris and Sheila were coming towards me, Sheila talking animatedly. Her hair was untidy and there was grass and mud on her skirt. She gave me a smile so bright and delightful that any feeling of reproach I had, faded.

'Darling, I'm so sorry I scared you,' she said, 'but after I telephoned I thought I saw Farring in the hall!'

'Did you, by George!'

'So I followed,' said Sheila, 'and he went to the cottage. Orson met him, and I heard Orson telling him that he was a fool to go out. Then I tried to find my way back and got lost.'

'Get those wet shoes off,' I said, gruffly. 'I'll get your slippers.'

When I got back Cris asked me what the doctor had said, and I gave him a report, although I was thinking far more about Farring's visit to the hotel.

It was possible that he had received the 'instructions' about which Orson had talked so much, and they included a visit to Downs House. If so, it meant that he had come to see someone here. It was not Seeley, I imagined, for the interview would have been in Seeley's room, which Cris and Anton had found empty about the time that Farring was in the house.

'What happened to Anton?' I asked.

'We've left him on guard,' said Cris, 'and we're as-

137

suming that Orson is in the enemy's camp until we know differently. I'll relieve him in the morning, and then you can have a spell, Ned. The best thing for us to do,' he added, 'is to have forty winks. We can't question Elizabeth yet.'

I was uneasy about leaving Sheila with Elizabeth, but I had set the catch of the window, and she had promised to bolt as well as lock the door. In any case, if there were any alarm, we would hear it. Cris was a lighter sleeper than I, and I felt much happier at having him with us.

As I dozed off, I reflected that the mystery was no nearer being solved, and that Webb would have to take official action before long. Cabinet Minister or no Cabinet Minister, three murders demanded the urgent attention of the authorities and there could not be much more hushing up. I thought a little worriedly about Anton's reaction; it was not pleasant to think that undue influence was being brought to bear. Then I dismissed the thought; Cris was right, this appeared the best way of tackling the business, and Webb had lost no time in getting the services of one who was probably the most brilliant and successful secret agent of the war, to help him. I was capable of doing what I was told and looking after myself in an emergency, and I had come to know most of the necessary tricks. Anton was capable, fearless and persistent, but neither of us was worth a row of pins without Cris.

There were no disturbances during the night, but about half past six there was a tap at the door, and both Cris and I woke up at once. The door opened, and Sheila came in, tying her dressing-gown about her. She was flushed with sleep and her eyes were still drowsy.

'She's conscious,' she said.

When we got into the other room, Elizabeth was sitting up, supported by pillows. Once again I was reminded of the despair which I had once seen in her eyes, and which was so like the desperation her father had shown.

Sheila went off to get some tea. Cris kept in the background, for she did not know him and neither of us wanted further complications, while I sat on the edge of the bed and took her hand.

'Well,' I said, 'we've won another round. You're all right. Did you see who it was?'

She spoke with an obvious effort.

'Yes. The—the man with the dark moustache. I—I was sitting in the dark, and I suppose I dozed off. I didn't know anyone was in the room before something was round my neck and I couldn't cry out and couldn't move. Who—who saved me?'

'We all had a share in it,' I said. 'But don't worry about saying "thanks", it's part of the job.'

She said: 'I don't know that I want to say thanks.'

I was so startled that I dropped her hand. She stared at me, tight-lipped, her eyes over-brilliant, and I wondered if she were more ill than I imagined. My expression must have affected her, for she said quickly:

'I don't really mean that. I—I'm tremendously grateful, but . . .'

Again she broke off.

'Has something else happened?' I asked, quietly.

'No, nothing else,' she said, 'except that I'm beginning to see it all so clearly. He's responsible for it all. I've fought against believing it. I can't really believe it now, but he's behind everything.'

'He?' I echoed, but I knew who she meant.

'My father!'

'I don't think anyone can be really sure,' I said

139

awkwardly. 'After all, when I saw him he seemed pretty cut up.'

She said: 'I haven't been fair to you, Ned. I had to put him first, but now I can't go on with it. I wouldn't mind about the collection, I would fight to help him keep it, but the murders—*three* murders. He must be mad!'

I said: 'What do you mean, you haven't been fair?'

'The man at the cottage isn't my father,' she said quietly. 'I've known all the time that he wasn't.'

19

I Feel Completely Crestfallen

I stared at her, unable to accept what she had said: the man *must* be Farring. Why, I had heard him talking to Elizabeth just as a man would talk to his daughter, and she had answered him quite naturally.

She went on, slowly: 'I knew from the moment I went into the room. He's too thin, and there are other differences which anyone who knew Father well would notice in a moment. Even his voice isn't the same. It's no use saying you don't believe it,' she added, as if she could read my thoughts. 'It's true. He's not my father. I don't know who he is, but I'll swear that he isn't Father.'

'But why didn't you say so?'

'I thought I might learn the truth,' she said.

'Does Orson know?'

'He *must*,' said Elizabeth, and bit her lips. 'He must

140

know; no one who knows Father well could make any mistake, and he's done a lot of business with him.'

I tried to speak calmly, as I asked: 'You do know Orson, don't you?'

'No,' she said. 'I'd never met him until I came here. That *is* true. I knew that he worked for Father, and so did several other people whom he didn't allow me to meet. He did a lot of business which wasn't done through the galleries, although I didn't take much notice of it. Now I think I know what it was.'

I did not even speak, and Cris's raised hand, exhorting me to silence, was unnecessary.

'He's been buying and selling smuggled and stolen art treasures for years,' said Elizabeth. 'Orson said the letter contained the list of smuggled goods which my father knew nothing about, but I think it contained something much more incriminating than that. I think he and Orson have worked together in these swindles for a long time, and they're prepared to do anything to save themselves from the consequences of it. I think this man pretending to be my father is here so that you and the police should think that my father is a sick man, and frightened out of his life, while really he is working against you. I think that Abbott and Forbes knew the truth, and they were killed because of it. I think all this pretence, all this talk about someone else of whom my father and Orson are afraid, is eyewash.' She began to speak more quickly, and with greater vehemence, carried away by an emotion too strong for her to resist.

'I think that the man with the dark moustache works for them, and that's why he let you attack him and didn't kill Orson. He had no intention of really doing so and only wanted to make it seem as if he intended to. I think he allowed you to go free that night, so that you could tell the police how nearly Orson had been killed.

141

And I think it was discovered that I knew this man was not my father, and he—and he . . .'

She broke off, and turned her head away.

If she really thought that her father had given orders for her murder, such a conviction was enough to cause this breakdown. I was sure that she believed every word she said, and she was in no frame of mind for argument, although there were one or two things which I thought she had forgotten.

I was glad when Sheila came in, carrying a tea-tray There was no point in staying, and I did not think it was necessary to say anything to Sheila, who saw at once that there was something the matter. So Cris and I left them together and went into the other room.

He was looking at me with a faraway expression in his eyes, one I knew well, and which I was sure meant that he would not hear me if I spoke.

He smiled suddenly.

'Well, Ned, what do you make of that?'

'She must know her own father,' I said, 'but I'm not sure she's reached the right conclusion.'

'So Farring still has a champion!'

'She's had a shock,' I said. 'Any girl who thought that her father deliberately ordered her to be killed would feel pretty grim about it, and it would prevent her from seeing things in a proper perspective. There are things which aren't explained by her theory, particularly about Orson. The other fellow, Seeley, *was* searching the house when I got there, it wasn't an act put on to deceive me. And Orson had a blow when the list was lost. If Orson and her father are working together, then the man with the black moustache wouldn't have come back to take the list just then.'

'Poor reasoning, Ned,' said Cris, cheerfully. 'They— there were two of them, weren't there?—might have

142

wanted you to think there are two factions when in fact there is only one. She could be right there. Seeley is a different matter, and he might represent a third party interest.'

'I suppose you're right there,' I said, reluctantly.

'So our interest is now centred on Seeley,' said Cris. 'There isn't much point in speculating about that. You know,' he added, looking at me as if he were about to pronounce some weighty verdict, 'I could do with a cup of tea!'

'Don't play the fool,' I said.

'I'm not fooling, and if Sheila can work a miracle, so can I. I wonder if there's any service yet?' He rang the service bell, and I stood looking at him, not a little exasperated by his behaviour.

A maid came, and promised to bring tea right away.

'This is certainly the most efficient hotel I've come across for a long time,' said Cris rather smugly. 'What were you saying?'

'I was trying to make you realise that this business is serious,' I said.

'As if I didn't know it! Ned, one question stands out a mile, you know.'

'What's that?'

'If this man isn't the genuine Farring, where *is* Farring?'

'Even I saw that,' I said, sarcastically.

'I don't think you're too happy in the early morning,' said Cris, 'your temper isn't what it might be. Ah, tea! That will brighten you up!' The maid came in, and Cris poured out tea.

He had been talking for the sake of it, and I knew that his mind was occupied with something different.

'Orson now,' he said. 'A likable fellow. Odd busi-

143

ness, Elizabeth and Orson—you think they're in love with each other, don't you?'

'If she's telling the truth, they can't be!'

Cris chuckled.

'One explanation is that she might still be deceiving us, another is that you have not a really romantic mind. Love at first sight, Ned! Surely you remember it!'

'Really . . .' I began.

'The trouble was that it took you several months to realise what had happened to you,' Cris went on reminiscently, 'but it happened almost at first sight. It *could* be the same with Orson and Elizabeth.'

'Even if you're right,' I said, 'it's very unlikely to affect him in the same way.'

'You mean that it's unlikely that both of them would feel an affinity within a few hours of meeting,' said Cris. 'I'm not so sure. I'm inclined to think, anyhow, that Elizabeth is just as cut up about Orson being a party to this strangling attempt as her father being in it.'

I shrugged my shoulders.

'You may be right, but I don't see that it matters much. By the way, who do you think was here last night —the real Farring or the false?'

'The man Sheila saw, you mean? Why ask me? The real Blundell or the false,' he added, more lightly than I thought was called for, 'and the real Farring or the false—we've two experts in disguises!'

'If you will persist in this tiresome mood,' I said irritably, 'I'm going to have a bath and shave. All I know is that if Elizabeth is right, and it's quite likely that she is, and if Seeley is the only outsider, then we can explain everything.'

'Phew! Everything!'

'Of course! The stolen collection, the faked one all ready to prove that it was in existence *after* the theft,

144

the burning of the stuff to make it a matter for insurance, probably a plan to collect insurance for the Arturo Gallery and to leave the real stuff with Farring. All the murder and mystery would be explained, too. As soon as Reccivi discovered that something was amiss, he had to be dealt with. The same with Forbes and Abbott. Farring plants an impersonator here to make his innocence clear to the world, and Orson pitches a fantastic story about Farring being gradually drawn into a criminal conspiracy, against his will, whereas if Farring is the man he's supposed to be, he would have gone to the police right away.'

'Ah,' said Cris.

'I am going to shave,' I said, abruptly.

I am not often irritated by Cris, but I thought he was being far too casual about the whole affair. I should have known that he had seen something which was hidden from me, although later, when I knew about it, I realised that I should have seen it too.

Just then, however, I felt disgruntled. Cris followed me to the bathroom, and we were still maintaining an undignified silence when we went down to an early breakfast.

It held fast until we were in the middle of toast and marmalade, but by then I'd had enough of it.

'Look here,' I said a little awkwardly, 'need we go on behaving like a couple of school kids?'

Cris grinned.

'Quite unnecessary, old chap. I had a bet with myself that you wouldn't keep it up after your second piece of toast. I've been waiting to ask you to go to the cottage and take the next watch for me. Keep an eye on Farring, and generally make yourself useful until I come over. Don't let Orson know that you're there, of course, and if he should discover it, don't tell him what Elizabeth has been saying.'

'I'm not likely to,' I said.

I thought that he was making amends handsomely, for he doubtless realised that I was anxious to find out whether there was anything at the cottage to justify Elizabeth's statements. I was in a better mood when I left Downs House, after telling Sheila that I would be back about lunch-time.

I reached the cottage by half past eight, feeling more than a little guilty, for Anton had been there for too long. I had seen the room in which he had his hiding-place, and I made for a ground-floor window, feeling quite confident that I was not seen.

The bedroom was at the end of a narrow passage, and I nipped along it fairly quickly.

There was no sign of Anton, which was not surprising, as he did not know who it was. I grinned to myself at the thought of him hiding in the wardrobe, not daring to look out, and tapped on the door.

'All safe,' I said, 'this is the relief party!'

There was no answer and no movement.

In sudden alarm, I pulled open the door; the wardrobe was empty.

20

Neither Friend Nor Foe

I stepped back from the open wardrobe, realising that if Anton had been spirited away from the room it would be as easy for the same thing to happen to me.

The trouble here was that we were never sure who was a friend and who was a foe; Farring—as I knew him—and Orson were neutrals, according to the way we had been accepting them, and the burly 'warder' was a colourless individual who had done nothing but accept orders.

Now very different thoughts crowded my mind.

If Elizabeth were right, the man whose name I did not know and whom I had once thought to be ex-aggeratedly disguised, was working with the people here, and therefore they had plenty of manpower. I was angry with myself for not having warned Anton the moment I heard Elizabeth's story. I think I would have done so but for Cris's presence; I had grown so accustomed to Cris making arrangements, and I sup-pose I had left everything to him.

It had been assumed that if trouble came to Anton he would reveal himself and make a bee-line for the telephone; as Orson, at that time, had been considered a friend rather than a foe. Now all my original doubts were revived. I could not make up my mind whether to go downstairs and announce my presence and demand that the others helped me to search for Anton, or whether to go back the way I had come, and tell Cris.

I decided to make a quick, furtive search of the cot-tage, and left the room, pausing near the stairs. I looked into two other bedrooms, leaving only that one where I had seen 'Farring' and then went downstairs. The first thing I heard when I reached the hall was Anton's voice!

'No, I will certainly not be sorry! Where is he?' There was a pause, and then the ting of a telephone receiver being replaced. As I approached the door of the study, Anton saw me before he came out of the room.

'Why, Ned! You've been very quick. Cris told me that you had only just left!'

'You scared me out of my skin,' I said, 'when I found the room empty . . .'

'Forget it,' said Anton. 'There was some trouble, and I came to see if I could help. It proved to be nothing more than the man who calls himself Farring throwing a fit.' He shrugged his shoulders, and went on quickly: 'Yes, I knew the truth about him, even before Cris told me over the telephone. In the fit he raved, and the truth came out then. I do not know who was the more surprised, Orson or I.'

'Where is Orson?' I demanded.

'In the dining-room,' said Anton, 'feeling very bewildered—or so he says.' He shrugged his shoulders. 'Everyone seems determined to spin lie after lie, to confuse us. If Orson is to be believed, then he was convinced that the man here was Farring, and if he is lying, he is a pretty good actor.'

'He's supposed to have known Farring for years,' I protested.

'Yes, I know. But go and argue with him yourself, Ned. I am too tired!' I could see that his eyes were glassy with lack of sleep, and so I saw him off, after he had told me that the 'warder', who also appeared to be a male nurse, was in the kitchen. Then I went along to see Orson. Anton had told him that either Cris or I would arrive, and he did not look surprised. He was obviously tired, and the way his jaw was set suggested that he was trying hard to keep control over circumstances which were proving too much for him.

'Come in, Deane,' he said, 'and try to help me work out this incredible business. Duval told you about the

148

man upstairs, I suppose?' When I nodded, he went on: 'I can hardly believe it, but I suppose it must be true. He was in delirium, and everything he said made it obvious that he's been masquerading as Farring for years.'

'*Years?*' I exclaimed.

'Yes, years,' said Orson, grimly. 'As far as I can gather, *I have never seen the real Farring.*'

I stared at him, open-mouthed.

'You might well look surprised,' he said. 'This fellow came to see me years ago, introduced himself as Farring and gave me all the necessary credentials. He told me that he preferred to keep this part of his business separate from the rest, gave me a private-line telephone number, and asked me not to visit his house. Whenever I've wanted to get in touch with him I've telephoned the number, and he's always paid me well—generously, in fact. Now . . .' He broke off, helplessly. 'Well, I suppose I shouldn't complain, the likeness even deceived his own daughter, and I've only seen newspaper photographs of him.'

He looked at me with something disquieting in his expression; I rated him at that moment as a man who was profoundly disturbed and unhappy. 'How the devil am I going to tell Elizabeth?'

I said nothing.

'She'll have to know, sooner or later,' he said, 'and it's quite obvious now that the real Farring is behind the whole bag of tricks. It will just about break her heart!'

He went on to talk on the same lines as Elizabeth had done. He drew the same conclusions about the obvious fact that Farring had been working illegally for many years, and had worked up this elaborate system of camouflage so that he should never be suspected—or, if he were suspected, that he would have a means of proving that he was not implicated. I said nothing. It all seemed quite clear, now, but I had one uncomfortable thought.

Everyone who knew that the man here was not Farring was in acute danger. If the man were prepared to murder his own daughter, he would not stop at me, or Orson, Cris or Anton. Elizabeth still remained in danger, and so did Sheila. The only ease to my disquiet was my conviction that Cris would realise it as soon as I did, and that he would not allow anything to happen at Downs House. Actually, Orson and I were in greater danger, because we were more isolated.

'Well, how *am* I going to tell her?' demanded Orson.

'I don't think I should worry about Elizabeth,' I said. 'I shall be surprised if she hasn't got some idea of it already. What about this nurse, or keeper, or whatever you call him? He must be in the racket, too.'

'He says that Farring—*this* Farring—employed him, and he doesn't know anything much about it,' said Orson, 'except that there is something crooked going on. He gets paid well and asks no questions. I've got the impression that he has a police record, and is too scared of the police to run to them with any tales. He's jittery now, because of the murder, but he's in much the same position as I am—he doesn't do anything about it, because he doesn't see what he can do. One thing is quite certain, though.'

'What's that?' I asked.

'You will have to make a full report to the police,' said Orson. 'Our earlier agreement is washed out, now. I thought I was protecting Farring. I'd carry on the way I was going if I thought it would help his daughter,' he added, 'but I don't see how it would, do you?'

'No,' I admitted.

I felt relieved. I had not seen the wood for the trees, but Orson had shown me by talking of the police. The situation had reached a stage where there was nothing we could do, and I was coming to the conclusion that nothing else would happen down here. The bogus Farring had served his purpose.

It dawned upon me that the whole business in Menlow had probably been started and carried out to distract attention from the real Farring and his activities.

That was the most uncomfortable thought, but I consoled myself with the fact that I had done everything I could, and the police had certainly fallen for it hook, line and sinker. What with my preoccupation, and Orson's glumness, the atmosphere of the dining-room was anything but cheerful. I tried to find out whether Orson had the faintest idea of the identity of the man with the black moustache, but he said that he was completely mystified.

The telephone bell rang during a period of silence. Orson went out, but called me after a few seconds.

'It's for you, Deane.' He handed me the receiver.

'Hallo, Ned,' said Cris. 'Have you seen anything of Seeley?'

'No, why?'

'He hasn't been in his room all night, though his car is in the garage. He hasn't been seen since dinner-time yesterday, but the manager doesn't seem to think that it's one of his usual business trips. Keep your eyes open for him, won't you?'

'Of course,' I said. 'Just a minute, Cris. I've been talking to Orson, who is of the opinion that we should tell the whole story to the police.'

'I have done,' said Cris, promptly. 'I've just been on the telephone to Webb, and there isn't much that he doesn't know now. I've told him that it looks to me as if

151

the affair down here was staged to distract his attention,' and that in all probability the real racket is being worked from somewhere else.'

'Well I'm damned!' I said.

'Of course you've thought of that,' said Cris. 'It's fairly obvious now, but I've an uncomfortable idea that Webb thought it all along!'

'Surely he wouldn't send us on a wild goose chase!'

'You could hardly call it that,' said Cris. 'Supposing he wanted the real Farring and the rest of the mob to think he was concentrating on Menlow, while he was actually working somewhere else? You couldn't blame him, could you?'

'I suppose not,' I admitted reluctantly.

'All this is guesswork,' said Cris, 'but . . .'

I said: 'Now look here, the attempted murder of Elizabeth wasn't guesswork, and that could only have been because she knew the truth about this Farring. Take my tip, and let everyone know that you've told the police everything, because if you don't the beggars might try to indulge in wholesale slaughter, to prevent it from leaking out!'

'Don't worry about that, Ned. I took care that most of my talk to Webb was overheard. By now the entire hotel probably thinks that we are all police agents.'

'Well, that's something,' I said.

As Cris rang off, I looked up to see Orson staring at me intently. For a moment he rather frightened me, and then I realised the explanation for his expression.

'Why wasn't I told that someone tried to kill Elizabeth?' he demanded, harshly.

'Oh, come,' I said, 'there's no need to look like that, no harm came to her.'

'I should have been told!'

He turned his back on me, snatched a hat from the

hall-stand, and went out. I watched him as he strode towards Downs House.

He was nearly out of sight when I heard something which was all too familiar. A shot rang out. I saw Orson hesitate, and then he swung round and flung himself down on his face. Another shot rang out. I took out my automatic. There were footsteps behind me, and I turned to see the 'warder'. He was a burly, ill-featured individual, and this time he appeared to be distinctly nervous.

'What's that?'

'Pigeon shooting,' I said.

A third shot broke through the quiet of the morning, and with a grunt the 'warder' fell to the floor.

For a split second I stood there like a fool. Then I dodged swiftly to one side, and as I did so another bullet hit the wall unpleasantly close. I saw Orson scramble to his feet, while I moved to the side of the house, opened a window and climbed out.

Bending low I hurried towards the hedge and peered over it cautiously, but two shots in succession made me withdraw my head. I did not think they were directed towards me, however, and I ventured out again. Trees were dotted about the ground, and taking as much cover as I could I moved towards the sound of the shots.

Then I came upon a clearing—and for a moment I stood quite still.

A rifle lay on the grass, and near it two men were fighting.

One was Seeley, the other was the man with the dark moustache.

I said sharply: 'All right, stop it!'

I don't know whether they heard me, and I went forward more quickly.

Orson came running up.

'That's enough!' I said, and I struck the man with the black moustache sharply on the head with the butt of my gun. He relaxed his grip on Seeley, which had all but strangled him, and then fell like a log. Seeley stood gasping for air with a sound like tearing silk.

'What . . .' Orson began.

I motioned him to silence. The man I had struck was stretched out now, and his eyes were closed. He was breathing convulsively, and I thought with bitter anger that he was now feeling something of Elizabeth's suffering the night before.

At last, I thought: Well, we've got two of them. There was some satisfaction in this achievement, although it was irritating not to be able to ask questions, for neither was in any shape to answer.

Then I remembered the little man who had been at Orson's house, and my satisfaction faded.

I said sharply: 'Someone else might be about, Orson, be careful!'

Seeley spoke for the first time, a gasp which I could only just understand. 'Over—there! Over—there!' I looked in the direction of his pointing finger, and although I could see nothing, I stepped forward, my gun cocked. Suddenly I saw someone else lying on the ground. As I drew nearer, I saw that it was the very man of whom I had been thinking.

As I looked down at him, I realised with increasing astonishment that Seeley had knocked him out and then started on the other. What was more, he had warned me of the possible danger.

'Who is it?' Orson demanded.

'The man I told you about the other night,' I said. 'Look here, cut along for Duval and St. Clare, will you, I can manage these.'

Orson said: 'Are you sure? No, wait a minute!'

He picked up the man as easily as he would a bag of potatoes, and carried him to the side of his companion. It was of course a much safer arrangement for me.

Orson went off with obvious reluctance while I kept Seeley covered, although I knew there was something here which would have to be explained. The suggestion that Seeley represented the third party and that the two men on the ground were working with Farring seemed the right one.

Seeley drew in his breath, and although his voice sounded reedy, his words were intelligible.

'Thank you, Mr. Deane. I . . .'

I moved my gun as he put his hand to his pocket. He hesitated and then said quietly:

'I wish only to show you my authority.'

'Authority?'

'Yes.' Quietly Seeley took out his wallet, while I kept him covered, half-prepared for a trick.

At arm's length he held a card out to me.

From the very beginning it had been a topsy-turvy business, and the things which I had least expected turned up, but nothing had surprised me as much as that card. I read it and re-read it, looked up at him and saw his smile, then looked down, and ran my hand across my forehead. I harboured evil thoughts of Superintendent Webb, too, for the card read:

Chief Inspector Arthur Searle
Criminal Investigation Department
New Scotland Yard, S.W.1.

21

A Step Nearer the Truth

'I'm afraid you're rather startled,' said Searle.

'Startled is one word,' I said, grimly. 'Why the devil was this—this *play-acting* considered necessary?'

'There's a good enough explanation,' said Seeley. 'I have been working on this case for some time, but I haven't got much further. It was thought that if someone could come down who was unofficially associated with the police, it would precipitate action, while there would be less chance of the villains in the piece finding out the truth about me.'

'I see,' I said. I was in no mood to accept that explanation or any other, for I was furiously angry, but I had the sense to realise that Searle was acting under orders, and also to realise that he had probably saved my life. 'Assuming it was necessary, what happened here?'

Searle said: 'I've been after this couple for some time, but it wasn't until last night that I discovered they have a kind of hut arrangement in the woods here. I spent a most uncomfortable night, waiting for them,' he added, 'and they didn't show up until half an hour ago, when they were both armed, obviously after someone. They loosed off a couple of rounds at Orson, and then turned towards you. The man with you was hit, wasn't he?'

'Yes,' I said, 'and killed instantaneously.'

'That's bad,' said Searle. 'Ruthless devils, aren't they?' He looked down at the two men dispassionately. 'We'd better make sure that they're not armed,' he went on, and ran through their pockets.

I kept them covered as he did so.

He brought to light two automatics and one nasty-looking knife, slipped them into his pockets, and straightened up.

'We'd better get them to the cottage,' I said. 'We can't keep them here.'

I was amazed at the change in the man I had known as Seeley. He looked the same, yet there was a different expression on his face, and the hint of furtiveness and unpleasantness had completely gone.

I gave up worrying about it, and as we walked towards the cottage, behind the two prisoners, I allowed myself to think with satisfaction of this new development.

As we stepped past the body of 'Farring's' 'warder' I spared a thought for the man upstairs, and as soon as the prisoners were in the study, I hurried up to make sure that he was all right.

He was in bed and asleep.

I could not help but stare at him. He was older than I had thought, and he looked ill. I wondered how on earth he had been induced to get himself into this position. Why had a sick man been allowed such comparative freedom of movement and action, when a single careless word from him would give the whole game away? How had he kept up the pretence with Orson for so long? How had he found the strength to maintain it with Elizabeth?

I was puzzled, too, because there had been no serious attempt to prevent me from seeing him. It was one of the features of the affair which I found most inexplicable.

I went downstairs again.

I had not been in the room with the others for more than a minute before I heard a 'view hallo' and, looking out of the window, saw Cris and Anton. I went to greet them, and together we carried the body of the warder to one of the bedrooms.

I then explained briefly what had happened, omitting Seeley's identity.

'Orson gave us an idea of what's been going on,' said Cris. 'I will say this for him—he seemed more concerned about Elizabeth than about himself. How did he behave when he was being shot at?'

'Sensibly,' I said. 'He didn't turn tail and run, but he took precautions.'

'Hm! What have you done with the trio of rogues?'

Then I broke Seeley's position to him.

At least I had the satisfaction of knowing that he and Anton were as astonished as I had been. Anton indulged in a few heated epithets concerning Webb, but after the first shock, Cris seemed amused. He greeted Searle with good humour and readily agreed to take charge of the prisoners while he went off to send in his report.

Searle' behaviour puzzled me, and I was prepared to believe that he might be a fake, but when I looked at Cris I saw that he either believed or pretended to believe in him.

He was looking at the man with the dark moustache.

'That was a policeman, as you have learned to your cost,' he said. 'The police have been behaving very curiously in this affair, and I would not normally expect them to leave us alone with prisoners. They must have a reason.'

The man said nothing.

'You don't feel talkative, perhaps,' murmured Cris. 'I think that the police expected that, and as they have a very great regard for the rules and regulations, which makes it impossible for them to deal with you as I'm going to, they left you to me.'

The man's lips tightened.

Cris went on: 'I have spent a lot of time in France and Italy, and I have seen a lot of the things which the Germans do to make reluctant people talk. I don't like the methods, but there are times when they are necessary, and I think this is one of them. Don't forget your position. You are in this cottage, and there is only a sick man upstairs, and no one who will give you any help. Anton, close the windows, will you? You'd better put up those blackout shutters, too, they'll keep the sound in. Ned, switch on the light.'

I did so, and Anton closed the window and put up the shutters. Cris stepped to the door and shut it, and then turned and regarded the others.

'Now this is where we start,' he said. 'First, what's your name?'

The man did not answer.

I thought his companion was more likely to talk, but Cris seemed intent on the leader. Suddenly he moved forward, and struck at the man, but the blow did not land; I don't think he intended it to. He put a hand in the fellow's pocket and drew out a wallet, which he tossed to me.

'Catch, Ned! See what it tells us.'

There was no information in the wallet, it held only a few pound notes and some stamps.

'No identity card?' Cris asked, mildly.

'Nothing helpful,' I said.

'In that case . . .'

He slapped the man's face this time, sharply, and enough to make the fellow gasp. I began to feel uneasy. The truth was that Cris would not use Nazi methods, but he would give every indication that he was about to

159

do so. I doubted whether that man with the light hair and the dark moustache and eyebrows was the type who would crack under such pressure.

'Your name!' barked Cris.

'What difference does it make?' the other demanded, and I have never seen such malignance in a man's eyes.

Cris said coldly: 'You haven't cottoned on to the idea. The police have left you to me. I am not soft-hearted, and in any case you've forgotten that four men have been killed in this business, and several other attempted murders have to be taken into account.'

'The worst you can do is hang me.'

'That just isn't true,' said Cris, with deceptive gentleness. 'You see, we were put on to this job because it was known that you might be obstinate.'

I thought: It isn't going to work.

The man said: 'My name's Bishop.'

'Well, that's a start,' said Cris, lightly.

'If you think I'm going to talk . . .'

'I *know* you are,' said Cris.

It is rather difficult to describe the atmosphere. Cris's manner was a curious mixture of gentleness and grimness, and the impression he gave was that he was quite prepared to adopt any method to get the information he wanted and that nothing would stop him from learning the truth.

'I won't wait much longer,' he said. 'Where is the real Farring?'

Bishop drew in his breath.

'I will tell you this. If you try to get at the truth, you'll uncover a scandal so big that you'll wish you'd never started it!'

'Ah,' said Cris. 'Nefarious activities of a Cabinet Minister, is that it?'

He waited to see the fellow's startled expression, be-

160

fore swinging round on the little man. The tactics were good, and I began to see how effective Cris could be at such a task as this.

'Where's Farring?'

'I . . .'

'Where's Farring?' roared Cris, and swung a left which missed by a fraction and made the terror more acute.

'He's . . .'

I thought we had it then, but Bishop was not beaten. I have never seen a man move more quickly nor with such effect. He flung himself at the little man and got his hands about his throat. There was a single howl of terror before they crashed to the floor in a struggling mix-up which made it difficult for Cris or Anton or I to separate them. I settled it at last by cracking the bigger of the two over the head again. The blow was too hard, for Bishop flopped out and rolled over, unconscious.

'He'll be all right,' said Cris, as he helped the little man to his feet. 'One at a time is enough. We may as well know your name,' he added.

'C-C-Colley!'

'And you know where the real Farring is,' said Cris.

'Yes, I—listen, mister, if I tell you, will you give me a break? I never . . .'

'You have been a party to all kinds of crime,' said Cris, 'but I'll do the best I can for you. We want results, not revenge. Where is Farring?'

'He's at Halle Grange,' said Colley, drawing in his breath.

It did not even dawn on me immediately, but Cris's eyes lit up.

'Well, well! The residence of . . .'

'Sir Lancelot Bridie!' I exclaimed, suddenly understanding. 'That's where the collection was stored, and from where it was supposed to have been stolen! And —great Scott, Cris Bridie *is* a Cabinet Minister!'

'Without portfolio, and on affairs which touch Italy,' said Cris.

22

A Change of Venue

'Well, now we're beginning to see why Webb was so discreet and why they've taken such pains to avoid scandal,' I said. 'Cris, we're in deep waters!'

'We've been in them for a long time,' said Cris, offering Colley a cigarette. 'We haven't finished yet, Ned.' He leaned back in a more comfortable position. 'Does Bridie know anything about this, Colley?'

'I dunno'

'Does he know that Farring is at Halle Grange?'

I thought that was a foolish question, but the answer proved that it was not.

'I dunno,' said Colley. 'I don't think so.'

'Is Farring a free man?'

'Strewth, no!' exclaimed Colley.

Once broken down, he talked freely enough, and Cris did not interrupt him. There was much that he did not know, but he was able to tell us that Farring had been a virtual prisoner at Halle Grange for several weeks, since he had been taken from the nursing home. Only a part of the huge house was occupied by Farring and the men looking after him, of course, and Sir Lancelot Bridie had not been in residence for over six months, because of his work abroad. Colley said that he had been to the place several times and had been one of those who had helped to move the original collection. He did not know who worked with Bishop at the big house; he himself was only allowed to go there after dark.

Colley admitted freely that he had a criminal past and that Bishop controlled several men, all of whom lived at or near Halle Grange. He seemed prepared to rely on Cris's promise of future lenient treatment, and was eager to give all possible details. He told us that Blundell had been killed because Bishop had seen him at Downs House and Cris in Menlow, and knew there were two separate men. Blundell had been waylaid, shot, and buried in Abbott's grave.

'Why take Abbott out?' I demanded.

'We had orders,' said Colley, 'but we was going to take Abbott further away, then we had to come back and keep a watch on you, so we dumped him.'

Cris said: 'Why was Abbott killed?'

'Bishop said we couldn't trust him,' said Colley. 'He was getting to know too much, mister. Same with the feller today—Bishop didn't trust him any more, so he shot him. Would 'ave shot you if you'd been there much longer!' He looked at me. 'I never did no shooting, Bishop did all that.'

I omitted to remind him that Searle had taken a gun from his pocket.

Cris said, thoughtfully: 'What caused things to happen so suddenly? There was no killing before, was there? The collection was stolen, and that was that.'

'I dunno what caused it,' said Colley, 'all I knows is that Bishop had orders, and got into a fine old stew. Strewth, proper worked up, he was! I reckon they got to know that the narks was around, but I never thought that Seeley was a split, no sir, I never did! I knew you was,' he added, looking at me again. 'I heard Orson talking about it to the old geezer upstairs.'

'What do you know about him?' asked Cris.

Colley tapped his forehead, and said succinctly: 'Barmy.'

He swore that he could tell us nothing more, and I believed him. In an aside I asked Cris whether he intended to try to get more information out of Bishop, but he shook his head.

'We could get it,' he said, 'if we went far enough with him, but I don't feel like going that far.' He added: 'I hope Webb lets us in on Halle Grange.'

It had not occurred to me until then that the police might want to take over, but I was on tenterhooks from then on until we saw Webb and Searle.

The massive superintendent drew up in a small car, climbing out ponderously.

'Good morning, Mr. Deane!'

'One day I am going to tell you just what I think about you,' I said.

'Nothing unkind, I hope, nothing unkind,' said Webb, his grin broadening. 'You couldn't expect me to tell you everything, could you? As a matter of fact, Mr. Deane, I think you've done wonders.'

'Now I suppose I have to start on Sir Lancelot Bridie,' I said.

That shook him, but he continued to smile until he joined Cris and Anton in the study. More policemen had arrived and taken charge of Colley and Bishop. Arrangements had been made for the dead man to be taken away in an ambulance. Two policemen went upstairs to stand on guard outside 'Farring's' room, and Webb said that a police doctor from Salisbury was coming to examine him.

'Well, now,' Webb said, 'where have we got to?'

As Cris told the story I was vividly aware of the time Webb had come to see me at the flat. Obviously he had known then of the suspicion attaching to Sir Lancelot Bridie, and I thought again that he should have given me some idea of the reason for his request. Now, however, everything, even Clyde's willingness to help, was transparently clear.

When Cris finished, Webb said slowly:

'Well, that's a very complete story, Mr. St. Clare, and I hope there won't be much left to do. We want to see the real Farring now, of course. If he is being kept a prisoner, then his daughter's fears that he is dishonourably implicated are groundless. It won't be long before we know, one way or the other.'

'Are you going to Halle Grange yourself?' Cris asked.

'I can't do anything else, now,' said Webb. 'I'll report the circumstances first, of course, but Searle and I will soon be off there. You don't want to have anything more to do with it, I hope? You've found out where Farring is, which is what we wanted to know. We weren't sure, you see, but I had an idea that this wasn't the real Farring.'

'We'd like to see it through,' said Cris stubbornly.

'Exactly how do you mean?' demanded Webb.

'You do want Farring alive, don't you?'

'Naturally,' said Webb.

'And you don't seriously think you'll get him alive if you make a raid yourself, do you?' asked Cris. 'He's the only man living who can tell us everything, you know, whether he's in the conspiracy or not. Colley gave only one reason for the murders: the dead men knew too much. It looks to me as if things have pretty well got to a head, and that they're killing off quite ruthlessly to make sure that there's no leakage of information.'

Webb hesitated.

'Well, yes. The trouble is, though, that I have no authority to go any further. Of course, if you . . .' He broke off, with a slow smile. 'I'm sure you understand me.'

'Withdrawal of police authority,' murmured Cris. 'Correct me if I'm wrong, but I have an uncomfortable feeling that now you think the dirty work has been done, you've decided we're dispensable.'

Webb shook his head.

'No, Mr. St. Clare, that isn't true, and I shall make quite sure that everything you and your friends have done will be reported. You see, now that I know beyond all doubt that Halle Grange is being used by these rascals, I can get a search warrant, and—well, you've said it yourself, you know—things are coming to a head, and I don't think these people will stop at very much. It's been dangerous enough up to now, but it will be far more dangerous from now on, and I don't think I'm justified in asking you to carry on. That's the simple truth, sir. You've done very well indeed, and I'm grateful. Now the really nasty work begins, and that's our job.'

'Nonsense!' said Cris. 'We're in it.'

'I see,' said Webb. 'I see. Well, I have no doubt that it can be arranged for you to go ahead. I ask only one thing of you, Mr. St. Clare. In fact, I must make it a condition.'

'Go on.'

'You must not take Miss St. Clare nor Miss Farring with you,' said Webb. 'I think it will be far too dangerous when you get to Halle Grange to risk their safety, nor will you want any additional anxiety. Will you give me that undertaking?'

'Certainly, and on this I absolutely agree with you.'

'Then I will see what I can do,' said Webb. 'There is a telephone here, I believe.'

I could not be sure whether he wanted us to go to Halle Grange or not, but he moved off to the telephone in the hall, and in ten minutes came back to tell us that the necessary permission had been given, presumably by the Assistant Commissioner at Scotland Yard.

Before we left, we saw the doctor who had arrived to examine Farring. He gave an explanation which immediately satisfied all the questions in my mind about the sick man. 'Farring' had been kept going for a long time on drugs, which had then been withdrawn. The symptoms were all in keeping with that condition. After a certain stage, heroin destroyed the mind, and a sudden withdrawal of the drug was always likely to set up acute illness followed by a mental collapse.

'Not nice people at all,' said Webb severely. 'Oh, I've forgotten to ask you what you think about Mr. Orson.' He looked from me to Cris, then back at me.

I said that I thought Orson was a victim of the conspiracy, and countered with a question of my own. Why had Searle visited the burned-out cottage, and looked in that particular desk? Searle himself answered: he had not been sure of Orson's position, and had taken the opportunity to look through his cottage. The old bureau was one which almost certainly had a secret hiding-place, and he had started to work on it when I had disturbed him.

'Why didn't you tell me who you were?' I demanded.

Searle smiled.

'Well, Mr. Deane, I wanted to confuse the other side, and with that end in view I thought it better that you were suspicious of me. I was most anxious not to let them know who I was. On one occasion Bishop nearly got in touch with me, to try to buy me off whatever I was doing—he was convinced that I was looking for the collection, of course, and thought that I was probably prepared to condone any crime.'

I had to be satisfied with that.

Back at Downs House, I gave Sheila a résumé of what had happened.

Orson was obviously far more concerned with Elizabeth than he was with what had happened at the cottage, and he showed only a perfunctory interest in the story. We did not tell him as much as I had told Sheila, and we gave out that we were returning to London. We were keeping the rooms on, we said, because Sheila and I hoped to come back to finish our holiday in peace.

Then we all got into the police cars, and drove away.

Suddenly I remembered that whoever had stopped us from staying in the village had given the hotel number, and that could not have been Bishop or Colley. Once I had thought it was Seeley, but that was now ruled out. The only man left was Orson, as far as I knew, unless someone else lived at Downs House and was involved.

I turned impulsively to Webb, and told him about it. He listened gravely enough but without surprise.

'I'm glad you thought of that, Mr. Deane, it's very interesting. Don't think that we shall forget to keep an eye on Orson and everyone else there, you needn't worry about that.'

'Good!' I said.

It was just after midday that we left for Halle, in a four-seater Buick which the police hired for us. Halle was only about seventy miles away, and we hoped to be there soon after three o'clock, allowing for lunch on the road. I was still confused and uncertain, but there was a great deal of satisfaction at being with Cris and Anton. Often we had gone forth to adventure not knowing what lay ahead of us, and although I could never capture the light-hearted joy in adventure of the others, I had never worried a great deal. Now Cris was singing gaily to Anton's whistling accompaniment, while I sat in the back and glumly watched the hedges and fields of Wiltshire.

We had lunch in Devizes, reached Cirencester just before three o'clock, and drove past the gates of Halle Grange at a quarter past three. The sun, breaking through cloud, shone on a great Georgian pile just visible through spreading beech and chestnut trees.

'*Voilà!*' cried Anton. 'We arrived at the scene of the mystery! Now tell us, Cris, what great plans you have evolved to deal with it!'

23

I Realise an Obvious Fact

Cris looked at Anton with a grin, then turned and looked at me. A small car travelling towards us in the middle of the road barely skimmed our wheel.

'Look at the road, confound you!' I said testily.

Cris pulled over.

'The great plan is elementary,' he said. 'We're going to visit the vaults.'

'How do you know there are any?' I demanded.

Cris laughed.

'I know Halle Grange pretty well,' he said, 'and I've been in the vaults several times. As a matter of fact my family and the Bridies have known each other for years.'

I sat back in astonishment; yet I should not have done. Cris's father had been on the fringe of Cabinet rank several times, and of course Halle Grange would be well known to him. In its way, it was a second Chequers, and there had been many informal conferences there. The more I thought of that the more incredible the whole business seemed.

'*Nom d'un nom*, now we learn!' cried Anton.

'Learn what?' I demanded.

'Why they were so glad to use us,' said Anton.

At first I had assumed that it was my acquaintance with Reccivi which had persuaded Webb to ask for help. Later I had decided that it was because we had worked so much in secret and were used to affrays of the type which were likely to develop at Menlow. Now I realised an obvious fact. Cris *knew* this house and the vaults, and no one could have been in a better position to work there.

'In my opinion, there's been a lot of unnecessary subterfuge,' I said. 'Nevertheless the fact that you know the house will certainly be an enormous help.'

Cris pulled up where the hedge was low and, looking in the direction of Halle Grange, we could see the spire of a church, which was built a little way away from the house itself.

'The vaults are under the west wing,' said Cris, dreamily. 'In addition there are several ventilation shafts, and if it came to a point we could get down through one of them.'

'Anyone hiding there could also get out that way,' I said.

'Well, well, what a pessimistic chap you are!' said Cris. 'We're here, and we haven't been spotted. Isn't that something? I think we'll wait until after dark and then visit the church and see whether the door from there to the vaults has been used lately.'

I said: '*Someone* has to stop flying balloons! Is there any sense in going down, even if we can find a way? Colley warned us that there are several men about, and presumably they're all quartered in the vaults. Why didn't you let the police raid the place in a straight-forward fashion, and just insist on us being in at the finish?'

Cris grinned.

'They prefer it this way, and they've good reason. I prefer it this way, too. Webb put up every possible objection, remember, quite enough to have dissuaded sensible people, but we insisted. Before, we worked at his request, now, we're working at our own risk, which is fair enough!'

'I suppose you're right,' I said, 'but there's something odd about it. I can't imagine Webb or anyone else not wanting to be in at the end of the show.'

'He'll be at Cirencester, as arranged, in good time,' said Cris, 'and it won't take them long to get here from there. Don't worry about support from the rear!'

I said no more, but I did not feel too happy. Anton seemed quite cheerful, however, as we drove along to a little village, where Cris pulled up in a lane while Anton and I went to inquire for rooms at the inn. We had no trouble in booking accommodation for the night. We gave false names, asked for dinner at seven-thirty, and then went back to the car.

In the short time that we had been away, Cris had used his make-up to advantage. Anton and I knew him well enough, of course, but no one who had only seen

171

him casually would have recognised him. Not until then did I realise that he had been a frequent visitor to Halle Grange.

We drove up a secondary drive, from the village, parked the car in a clearing where it could not be seen casually, and then roamed through the grounds. All three of us were experts at moving about without attracting attention, but it was odd to be in an English wood, in such circumstances.

Cris decided against exploring the church. Visitors were not unknown, even when the family was not in residence. We did no more, therefore, than reconnoitre the grounds. Cris took us to three places where there were ventilation shafts; all of them coming out along the banks of a stream. The shafts were heavily camouflaged by bushes and had obviously not been used for some time. It was clear that whoever had taken possession of the vaults either did not know of their existence, or else had not worried about them.

We got back to the inn in good time for a surprisingly well-cooked meal.

We did not hurry over it, and by the time we had finished, it was nearly dark. Undeterred we went out once again, this time on foot. Before leaving, all of us checked our guns and made sure that they were loaded, and each had two spare clips of ammunition. By the time we reached the church it was quite dark.

The door was locked, but Cris did not take long to open it.

We walked quietly through the nave to the sacristy where Cris examined the oak panelling while Anton was dispatched to lurk outside the door, ready to warn us if anyone should come along. Cris seemed to be a long time, but at last he stopped, turned and nodded, his face looking strange in the half-light.

There is nothing unusual about tunnels and secret entrances in old houses, but I admit I had a thrill as one of the panels slowly opened. Beyond, there appeared to be only a dark cavity, until I shone the torch further into it and saw a flight of narrow stone steps.

Anton was recalled, and we all looked as far down the steps as we could. There was not the fusty smell that I had expected, and I took it to mean that the entrance had been used, or else that the ventilation was excellent.

'Well, what next?' asked Anton.

'One of us should stay up here,' said Cris. 'Ned, would you mind?'

As Anton had had the rough end of the stick until then, I raised no objection, although I envied them as they went down cautiously, Cris leading the way. Their footsteps made little sound, and soon there was only a brooding silence and the darkness around me.

The others seemed to be away a long time.

I thought over all that had happened, and the amazing fact that we had come to this place. I was quite sure that Cris was right; we had been asked to help because of his special advantages here. Whether that were justification for the way in which the affair had been handled was a different matter, for Webb's high-handedness still rankled with me.

I had been there for over half an hour, watching the face of my illuminated watch every few minutes, before I heard sounds from the staircase. I crept to the doorway. Cris's voice came to me, faint and sepulchral.

'All clear, Ned?'

'Yes,' I whispered.

When they joined me, they were breathing heavily. It was some time before Cris spoke, and then it was in a voice less carefree than before.

173

'They've blocked up the main entrance to the vaults from this side. We can't get in.'

'How is it blocked?' I demanded.

'Cement,' said Cris, grimly. 'I've been chasing around trying to find a secondary way in; I know there used to be one, but I haven't found it.'

'I suppose you want to break in now,' I said, gruffly.

'Now or later,' said Cris. He paused. 'The only other way would seem to be by one of the ventilation shafts. Are you game to try?'

'I suppose so,' I said.

Anton said: 'What about me? I'm thinner, and perhaps . . .'

'For heaven's sake keep your voices down!' said Cris suddenly. 'We're supposed to be on a secret expedition.'

We all stood still but no sound of discovery came to our ears. Much subdued, we crept back and made our way in single file to the stream.

We reached one of the bushes.

Here Anton took a false step and found himself ankle deep in water. Muttering bloodthirsty imprecations, he climbed to the bank again. After that little mishap we waited until silence was all about us. Then Cris began to work on the grille of a ventilator shaft. He worked deftly, but it seemed to me that there was every likelihood the screws had rusted and the heads would break off. Cris persevered, however, and at last got one screw out.

With infinite patience he tried again.

It must have taken an hour before the grille was lying on the bank and I was directing my torch into the shaft itself. I could see moss on either side, and water dripping from the top.

'It's all right,' said Cris encouragingly. 'Once we're

through the opening it gets bigger. For God's sake keep the light steady.'

He slithered in, his head bent low.

Anton went next, and being slimmer, made a quicker job of it. I followed, and it was not an easy task, for I had to pull the grille back into position. It was done, however, and I crawled after the others.

There was an unpleasant smell of rats and damp, and the sides of the shaft were slimy. Viscid growth hung downwards, casting grotesque shadows. Every step carried with it the risk of slipping. It occurred to me that the shaft should be kept much cleaner than this, to do its job effectively. Then I recalled the cold, clean-smelling air which had come from the stairway leading from the chapel.

I suppose we slithered along for ten minutes before we came to a halt. In front of us there was a heavy wooden door, iron-studded, and, at first sight, impregnable. There was a keyhole, however, and the lock itself was not complicated. I held the torch again while Cris did the work. The noise the lock made as it moved was over-loud, and we stood waiting with fast-beating hearts.

No alarm was raised, however.

I tried to tell myself that it was quite possible that no one was in the vaults, and in any case I had an impression that they were so large and divided into so many compartments that noise at one end would not be heard at the other. It did not make me feel any less apprehensive, however, as Cris pulled the door open and we stepped through into the passage beyond.

Twenty yards further along, probably a hundred yards or more from the bank of the stream, we came upon another grille, built into the wall on a level with my shoulders. Cris set to work at once, but it took some

175

time before he had the grille out, and, with Anton's help, put it against the wall. Then Anton climbed up on my shoulders as I knelt down.

He whispered: 'There is a wall a foot thick, and then another grille.'

'Where are the screws?' asked Cris.

'On the other side.'

'Too bad,' said Cris. 'All right, come back.'

As Anton slid down from my shoulders, I straightened up with a grimace. Then Cris found that by turning on his side he could get his head and shoulders into the hole, and if Anton and I supported his waist, manage to work on the steel with a saw-blade. My heart dropped, for it meant a long session, but there was nothing else to do.

After a lot of experimenting, we found that the most satisfactory way was for Anton and I to take it in turns to sit on the floor so that Cris's legs could rest on our shoulders, while the other gave him some support about the waist. From then on there seemed to be an interminable period of quiet broken only by soft, rhythmic sawing. Anton and I changed places three times before Cris gave it up, and Anton took his place. He was not able to stand working in that cramped space for so long, and Cris wanted to go back, but I insisted on taking my turn, although I have broader shoulders than either of the others, and it was a tighter squeeze.

By resting the torch in front of me, I could see the grille easily enough. Several of the bars were already cut through, but it took an interminable time for me to cut through another. For some reason the next was much easier. By that time, however, I was suffering so severely from cramp that I had to give up.

Cris lost no time, and got to work again immediately.

It was now nearly midnight, and the chances of being discovered should be less.

Cris began to wriggle backwards, and when he joined us there was a lighter note in his voice.

'Not much longer,' he said, 'the bottom bars are so rusty they should be easy enough. You ought to see it through, Anton.'

He was too optimistic, for it was I who had the satisfaction of sawing through the last bar. That is, satisfaction when I started on it. It was short-lived, for I had not reckoned on the saw biting through so quickly, and before I could do anything to stop it, the whole grille had slipped from my fingers and dropped to the other side.

The din it kicked up was like an explosion. It seemed impossible for that noise to go unheard if anyone were in the vaults.

I was stuck there, my elbows jammed against the side, my head buzzing with the clattering din. It was some time before the others could draw me out, but there was not a word of reproach, only a tense, almost breathless silence. We stood like statues for what seemed a long time, until the last echo had faded and we could hear no sound at all. Then Cris drew in his breath sharply.

He hoisted himself up and squeezed through the opening, but before long he moved his feet twice, a signal for recall. When he got back, he said:

'The drop's too deep for head-first. Give me a hand.'

We lifted him, feet first, easing him through the hole until only his head and shoulders were left. Gradually he wriggled through and disappeared completely. His voice, like something disembodied, came back to us:

'All safe!'

Anton went next, and I brought up the rear. Then we were all three standing inside the vaults, amid a heartening silence.

24

The Vaults at Halle Grange

'There used to be a system of lighting,' said Cris.

He directed the beam of his torch round the walls. until it came to a doorway and, sure enough, there was an electric light switch close by. The light was subdued, and came from a single lamp in the middle of the ceiling, and by it we could see that the room was quite empty, and about twelve feet square.

Cris tried the door.

As I watched him I reflected that if we came across anyone, we were enough to frighten the life out of them. We were green with slime from the sides of the shaft, our faces were smeared with the beastly stuff, and some of the iron filings had stuck to our skin.

I said: 'That door's going to stop us.'

It was of steel and looked exceedingly heavy. Although there was a narrow keyhole, I could not see any chance of picking the lock. My spirits dropped, but Cris turned his head and grinned.

'Not it! Watch!'

I kept forgetting that he knew the place and the way in which the vaults were safeguarded. When we were in the next room he had told us that a secondary system of locking and unlocking the doors from the inside had been installed, so that there was no risk of anyone being locked in by accident. The door which had looked so impregnable actually proved our easiest task, for Cris found the right button, which was part of the electric light switch, and then we were able to slide the door to one side.

Cris waited for at least a minute, then switched on his torch, found the light switch, and pressed it down.

I gasped: 'Great Scott!'

'*Nom de Dieu!*' exclaimed Anton.

We gazed on a scene not unlike that at Orson's cottage. There were packing cases, some of them open, some with pictures resting against them. A few silver pieces were gleaming in the bright light, and near the farther door was a silver table, a wonderful piece of work, with exquisite moulding for which only Milanese craftsmen of the fifteenth century could have been responsible. That odd and inconsequential thought passed through my mind as I looked about me, knowing that we were standing in the midst of part of the Arturo Collection.

.   .   .   .   .

'So we have really found it,' said Anton, super-fluously. 'It's . . .' He broke off, at a loss for words.

'We haven't finished yet,' Cris said.

There was another door, which he opened in the same way as the last one. I expected to find pitch darkness ahead, and was startled when I saw a glow of light. We stood in the doorway, scarcely daring to breathe, listening.

After a minute of complete silence we crept forward towards the light.

It came through an open doorway, and was sufficient

179

to show that this room, also, was filled with treasures. I had not really recovered from the shock of finding the collection here, although what I expected to find I hardly know. By the time we reached the next door. however, I was fully occupied with the question of what we were going to do next.

The light was in a passage.

Later, I discovered that the vaults were a series of rooms connected by passages. The treasures were still, for the main part, in their packing cases, and the impression I had was that this was so to facilitate the collection being moved at short notice.

From the passage several doors opened, and all of them were ajar. We approached the light cautiously, Anton staying near one door, in case it or any of the others should open wider.

Cris and I were near the head of the passage when we heard footsteps. I raised a hand in warning, and Anton slipped into one of the rooms. Cris and I did the same. Then from a doorway we saw a man walk along the main passage. He was a hefty fellow, not unlike the murdered 'warder' at the cottage, and I guessed that he might be a night watchman. I was mostly concerned in case he came into our room, but he went on.

I peered after him—and saw with a shock that he had turned into Anton's room!

I touched Cris on the arm, and went out, walking as swiftly as I dared without making a noise. The man appeared not to have seen Anton, but suddenly I heard a gasp. I reached the room and hurried in, but I need not have worried, for Anton had managed to get a stranglehold on the fellow.

Cris knocked him out with the butt of his gun.

'One,' said Anton, with satisfaction.

I said: 'Quiet!' Then, as my heart beat fast and I

looked from one to the other, I added: 'Surely you can see what this means!'

Cris drew in his breath.

'Yes, we've got to go on with it now,' he said, 'but one of us must go back to make sure the police are alerted.'

I felt a sharp sense of disappointment.

He was quite right, of course, but I hated the thought of going back and missing whatever was to happen here. Anton must have thought exactly the same as I did. I imagined that Cris would give the verdict, but instead he said:

'Break three matches, Ned.'

I did so, hardly conscious of the room in which we were standing—it was a bedroom with two camp beds. I made sure that the matches were of different lengths, and as I held them I felt sure that I would be the unlucky one.

'Shortest one goes,' said Cris.

He drew the longest.

Anton shrugged and took one of the other two. We opened our hands. At first glance there did not seem to be much difference, but when we held them together, Anton's proved to be the smaller.

He went off with a fairly good grace. Cris and I looked at the unconscious man. Cris, who is always fully prepared for any emergency, brought a length of cord from his pocket, and we bound the man so that he could not possibly get himself free, then tied a handkerchief over his mouth. The main risk was that he might be due back at a certain time, or else that a second man would come to join him.

We decided not to venture out of the passage until Anton had had time enough to get to the village.

It was then half past one, and we were not looking

forward to the next hour, but we had to face it. We went into the other rooms, but two of them were empty and the third was another bedroom, not unlike the one we had already looked in. We stuck out the waiting period, and after Anton had been gone an hour we ventured into the next passage.

Several doors opened from this one, too.

Two rooms were stored with more of the collection; the third door was shut.

In that particular part of the vaults it was the first door we had come across that was closed. I wondered whether we were wise to try to open it but Cris took out his knife, selected the skeleton key blade, and set to work.

It was not particularly difficult. A bed was in it, and on the bed lay Leonard Farring.

·   ·   ·   ·   ·

There could be no doubt this time.

Farring was sound asleep, and did not move when we approached. I wondered if it were a drugged sleep, but there was no point in speculating.

'Close the door,' whispered Cris.

I closed and locked it, using the skeleton key, for the door key was missing.

'Now we'll know what it's about,' said Cris.

The man stirred.

'Wake up, Farring,' whispered Cris. 'Wake up . . .'

Farring opened his eyes and started up; he looked terrified at first, but after a while the terror gave place to amazement.

'We're friends,' Cris whispered. 'Don't make a noise.'

'Who—who are you?'

'Friends of your daughter, you've nothing more to worry about.'

'Elizabeth! They—they told me she was dead!'

'She's very much alive,' said Cris, briskly. 'Now tell us what time someone is likely to come.'

Farring drew in his breath.

'They—they usually come about seven. I . . .'

He broke off, and drew a trembling hand across his forehead. I judged from his pallor and lacklustre eyes that he had been kept down here for a long time. The terror he had shown when he had first woken up was not simulated. He was a victim, there was no reasonable doubt of that.

Cris said: 'Listen to me, Farring. There has been crime and violence, and brutal murder, and we've got to get to the bottom of it. If you have anything to hide from the police . . .'

'*I* have nothing to hide,' declared Farring, in a stronger voice. 'Are you policemen? If so, you must prevent them from doing this thing. At all costs it must be stopped!'

'Keep your voice low,' urged Cris. 'What thing do you mean?'

'The whole collection is to be shipped abroad,' said Farring. 'Everything is going to America. I am supposed to have sold it, I, with whom it was left as a sacred trust.'

'They can't ship it now,' I said.

'They have all the papers prepared,' said Farring. 'I know they expect to take it away within forty-eight hours. I think it will leave the country before the end of the week. You *must* prevent it!'

'We will,' said Cris, confidently.

Farring gripped his arm. I was appalled by the thinness of the dealer's fingers and the way the bones showed.

In silence we waited for words that he was trying to say. Otherwise I doubt whether we would have heard the almost soundless opening of the door.

I swung round, with a gun in my hand. Cris stepped quickly to one side of the door, and I to the other.

It was a long time opening. Whoever was there did not come in at once.

Footsteps echoed along the passage and the man in the doorway, still out of sight, turned and spoke to whoever it was.

'The light is on and Farring's awake.'

'Go and look inside,' said the newcomer.

I don't know why it came as such a shock; I should have been prepared for it, and when I went into the whole business afterwards I realised that there was no other person who could have been responsible for that crime. Yet as I heard the voice I started in surprise, and even lowered my gun.

'Go and look inside!' repeated the newcomer, and the voice was Orson's.

25

The Reason for Discretion

I could not see Cris, because the open door was between us, and I was not sure what to do. I glanced at Farring, noting his wild-eyed terror-struck expression.

There was a moment of hesitation before the door was finally flung open.

Cris fired.

The shot sounded very loud, much louder than Orson's gasp. I heard him fall. I reached the passage just behind Cris.

Then an answering shot rang out.

Cris spun round as if someone had seized his shoulder, and staggered against the wall. I backed a pace. There was another man at the end of the passage. I did not recognise him, but I heard another shot, and the bullet hit the wall not far from me. I fired, and missed, fired again and, I think, scored a hit.

Another shot struck the wall near me, and I backed a little further into the room. I did not turn round, but I could hear Farring's heavy breathing, and I thought he was getting out of bed. Cris moved, and began to get up.

'Down!' I snapped, and thank God he heeded me, for a bullet hit the wall just above his head.

'There's a switch at the corner,' muttered Farring.

'No one can get past,' I said.

'There are several of them,' gasped Farring.

Orson drew in a deep breath, and said harshly:

'You won't live to see your triumph, Deane. If you show yourself you'll be shot, if you let my man get much further along the passage, he'll find a switch.'

It was all so unreal that I was not really sure that he was telling the truth. It was Farring's agonised voice which convinced me, as well as the sneer on Orson's face. I remembered what Bishop had said, how sure he was that we would never get the collection.

I edged towards the passage. A shot passed me. I saw the other man coming along the passage stealthily, pressed against one wall. Orson shouted to him to hurry. Another shot hit the ground just in front of me, and I

185

could feel chippings of cement as they struck upwards. I saw that the man was close to an ordinary light switch, with his right hand holding the gun and his left stretched out towards the switch.

I fired and flung myself forward. I missed with the shot but I gained time, for the bullet went so close that he dodged back. I hit the ground heavily, the wind knocked out of me, and I remember thinking that I had taken my chance and failed, for the gun was knocked out of my hand.

Then I heard a louder shot, and the flash of flame seemed to be right in front of my eyes. It was, for Cris, although on the floor and wounded, had fired towards the man. Afterwards, when I saw the state of his right forearm, I marvelled that he had been able to take aim and to hold the weight of the gun. Hardly had the flash died away before the man near the switch dropped to his knees, and then plunged forward. I heard Orson cursing as, still gasping for breath, I picked myself up and edged along to make sure that there was no further danger.

I need not have worried, for the man was dead.

. . . . .

Anton and the police arrived just after four o'clock. I suppose, everything considered, that they did not do so badly. The first arrivals came by way of the ventilation shaft, led by Anton. Others had gone to the front of the house, and had had some difficulty in finding their way to the vaults. The man who admitted them, Sir Lancelot Bridie's secretary and estate manager, was put under arrest right away; there was no evidence just then that he was implicated, but it was either the secretary or Bridie who had allowed the vaults to be used,

186

and Webb hoped for the best. He was justified; Bridie knew nothing at all of what was taking place. He had put the highest trust in his secretary, who had sole charge of Halle Grange during his absence, and the whole plot had been arranged by the secretary and some members of the household staff—recent acquisitions. The few old and loyal servants had been transferred to Bridie's house in Scotland. It transpired that for some months past Halle Grange had been used as a storehouse for the collection, Orson and those who worked for him, entering after dark, so that the suspicions of the gardeners and gamekeepers were not aroused.

Investigation uncovered a charge of T.N.T. beneath the floor, which would have wrecked the vaults and the house above it.

One of the astonishing features of that fantastic night was Farring's behaviour. After the first shooting he looked like fainting, and I had given him a little whisky out of my flask. But after ten minutes' rest Farring had got up, put on his dressing-gown, and then roamed the vaults, a man beside himself with joy.

He had been convinced that the collection would either be taken abroad or else destroyed. He told me, while I was helping to bandage Cris's arm, a lot of what had happened.

It appeared that the whole thing had started many years before.

Orson had been employed by him as an excellent copyist and restorer. The germ of the plot must have been planted then. Seeing the collection, handling some of it, Orson had planned, as I suspected, to murder the real Farring and to let the drug-ridden fellow at the cottage be known as Farring. Thus he would have escaped responsibility, for the drug-addict's mind would have been destroyed by heroin, and he could not have pleaded for himself. As far as Orson was concerned, at one time such a plot had looked foolproof. The only serious danger had been when Elizabeth had discovered that the man was not her father.

Orson had arrived at the vaults a few hours before, told the real Farring that his daughter had been killed because she had discovered the truth, and told him that he was likely to die at any moment. I remembered Orson's brilliant acting when he had 'heard' of the attack on Elizabeth, and knew that there was a sadistic streak in the man which had driven him to add to Farring's torment by saying that Elizabeth was dead.

To go back a little, to Farring's story.

After some time he had discovered that Orson was selling copies, as originals, to American buyers. They were very good copies, and few of them were found out. Orson branched out, employing craftsmen to make other art treasures which looked like genuine pieces. He had worked in antiques, sculpture, pictures and *objets d'art*, and his business had been tremendously successful.

From the very beginning, however, Orson had schemed to get the Arturo Collection. He had a buyer in America, a multi-millionaire, the revelation of whose name would cause something of a sensation in the United States, for Orson had a letter from him offering to buy the whole Arturo Collection *at any price and in any circumstances*. That was the letter which had been in the bureau at the cottage, the letter which Orson had pretended implicated the genuine Farring, and which had been stolen from me so easily.

When the bombing of London had started, Farring had wanted to get the collection out of danger, so he had arranged with Sir Lancelot Bridie to transfer it to the vaults of Halle Grange. Then, after Bridie had gone abroad on one of his many missions, the 'burglary' had been staged. Actually Orson, working with the secretary, had simply moved the collection to a little-known part of the vaults. The vans and the false credentials were all part of the bluff to make Farring, and, perhaps, the police, believe that the collection had been taken away from Halle Grange.

Orson had begun his elaborate scheme to get the collection shipped abroad and into the hands of the American multi-millionaire, and at the same time have Farring blamed for the theft, if it were ever discovered. With that object in view, he had planned the creation of the false collection. He had not minded my seeing it; he intended to make it look as if Farring himself had arranged it, and he had pitched his plausible story so that he himself appeared as a loyal friend of Farring.

Then Orson had needed money.

The craftsmen he employed had been quick to sense that there was something dishonest afoot. Their demands had gone up accordingly. Silence had to be paid for, and it asked, and got, a high price.

It was some time before we learned everything about what had happened at Menlow. Orson had been on edge when Searle arrived, but believed that Searle was an unscrupulous under-cover buyer, without suspecting that he worked for the police. He had kept a careful watch on Elizabeth, and thus soon discovered my purpose. For as long as Elizabeth thought the man at the cottage was her father, everything seemed all right for him, but he let her see him, knowing that I would arrange it somehow if he made difficulties: If she saw through the deception, then he expected to be able to frighten her into silence—as, in fact, he had for a while. He had trouble with Abbott, who wanted more money, and decided to kill him. He knew Searle was in the grounds, and Bishop did the shooting, hoping that Searle would be blamed; the gun used was actually found in Searle's room!

Blundell had been murdered for the reason which Colley had already given—in mistake for Cris.

By his clever acting, Orson had made me think that he was genuine. He had played on one of the most curious features of the affair to strengthen that impression—the passion which he inspired in Elizabeth from the first time she saw him. Later, he had arranged for Bishop to shoot at him in the woods, so that the finishing touch was put to his pretence of innocence. It had completely deceived me!

Webb, of course, was able to put in some odds and ends. In the main, he had told the truth when he had said that the reason for discretion was the fact that Sir Lancelot Bridie appeared to be implicated. The murder of Forbes had jolted him, but Reccivi's visit to me, added to the fact that I was not inexperienced, had seemed a god-send. In the circumstances, of course, Clyde had not hesitated to send for Cris. His knowledge of Halle Grange and its vaults had obviously made him the first choice.

The crop of murders had made it necessary to move very quickly. Webb had been prepared to raid the Grange, but had been afraid of the consequences. So he had let us come on ahead, after raising his objections and making the danger quite clear to us.

'So you didn't think we could be trusted to take a chance, knowing everything,' I said. We were then at the inn in Halle village, the following morning.

'I could not have let you go, had you known everything,' said Webb, with an apologetic smile. 'But I could see no other way of getting it done. Had the police come with you, Orson or the men there would have learned about it. You see, I knew that Orson was prepared to destroy everything directly the police were known to be suspicious of Halle Grange.'

'I suppose you can't be blamed,' I said, a trifle grudgingly.

Webb gave a conciliatory smile.

'It was all done for the best, I do assure you, and see how magnificently you succeeded.'

Anton said: 'There is one thing which *nothing* can explain, nothing at all.'

'You mean, who set fire to the fake collection?'

'Exactly! Who did? Everyone is now accounted for, and yet none of them would have done that. Unless, perhaps, Searle,' Anton added, looking at Webb.

'He wouldn't have done a thing like that,' said Webb, rubbing at his nose. 'It was arson, after all.' He looked at us with a cheerful innocence that was a little too good to be true. 'But believe me, *I'm* not worried about who did it, I'm quite prepared to believe it was another trick of Orson's.'

Webb went off soon afterwards. Farring, Anton and I stayed at the inn, for we were expecting Sheila and Elizabeth. They arrived about midday. Elizabeth knew the truth, but the shock of the discovery of Orson's true part in the affair was softened by relief at finding her father. She went into his room, after greeting me warmly, and Anton, Sheila and I went for a stroll towards the Grange. Anton told her what had happened, exaggerating my own part in it, as he nearly always does, and when he had finished, he said:

'Only one mystery remains, Sheila! That is, the fire. I have battered my brains, and I cannot imagine who did it!'

'Can't you?' asked Sheila quietly.

'Do *you* know?'

'Of course, but do keep it from the police. It was Elizabeth.'

'But why on earth . . .?'

'She was sure her father was guilty, and thought that a fake collection prepared on his orders would damn him,' said Sheila simply. 'Naturally the best thing to do was to get rid of it.'

I said: 'Well, now I know what Webb meant! I'm beginning to like that man!'

I liked him even better when, after we got back to London and Sheila and I were once again about to start a two weeks' holiday, Webb rang up to tell me that Reccivi was on the mend, and to apologise for not having arranged for the car which I had asked for; I said I'd forgotten it, and that it hadn't been needed, anyhow.

'I know, I know,' said Webb, 'but you never know what might happen, do you? I'm arranging for one to be placed at your disposal for the next fortnight!'

He chuckled as he rang off.

If you would like a complete list of Arrow books please send a postcard to
P.O. Box 29, Douglas, Isle of Man, Great Britain.